DEATH IN THE DARK

Eric Weiner has written numerous young adult thrillers and has also written for children's television. He lives in New York with his wife and son.

Death in the Dark

Eric Weiner

*Hodder
Children's
Books*

a division of Hodder Headline plc

First published in the USA 1995
by Harper Paperbacks, a division of HarperCollins*Publishers*

First published in the UK 1995
by Hodder Children's Books

A Catalogue record for this book is available
from the British Library

ISBN 0 340 65145 8

Typeset by Avon Dataset Ltd, Bidford-on-Avon

Printed and bound in Great Britain by
Cox & Wyman, Reading, Berks

Hodder Children's Books
a division of Hodder Headline plc
338 Euston Road
London NW1 3BH

CHAPTER 1

"JENNY SILVER'S MISSING."

"What?"

"She's missing. Gone. Vanished. No one's heard from her for three days."

I struggled up on one elbow. "What?" I said again.

"Did I wake you?" Candace asked.

"No, no, no."

"You sound half-asleep."

"Do I? Uh, what time is it?"

"One."

One. In the morning. That was Candace all over. Candace was my freshman roommate at Barnard. Starting tomorrow, she would be my sophomore roommate. She was thin and pretty; she was also a total dynamo. She never seemed to need any rest, and she assumed that the rest of the world operated the same way. No matter what the hour, she always acted surprised to find someone sleeping.

"Mrs. Silver just called me, so I just found out myself," she said. "She was pretty hysterical, as you can imagine. Actually, I *can't* imagine. Poor Jenny!

1

Poor Mrs. Silver!"

"She just called you now?"

"Did you hear what I said? Jenny's missing! Missing!"

"Oh God," I said. My heart was pounding hard. I guess the news had finally sunk in all the way. "You know what? If it was anyone but Jenny, I'd be really worried, but—"

"What are you talking about?"

"Oh, come on, you know how scatterbrained she is."

Last year Jenny Silver had lived in the room across from ours. She had cute red bangs and a spray of dark freckles across her apple cheeks. She was almost always cheerful and she was popular with guys. She was also the most absentminded girl I had ever known.

It was a running joke on our floor how often Jenny forgot her keys. Seemed like you'd always find her sitting in the hall humming along to her Walkman while she waited for one of her roommates to come home and let her in.

"So?" Candace said. "So she's a little spacey. What does that have to do with it?"

"A little spacey? Candace, she probably forgot where she lives."

"Ellie, do you have any idea how callous and gross you sound right—"

"Or maybe she went off somewhere, you know, without telling anybody where she was going."

"No. No, no, no, no. No."

"Candace," I said, "don't just say no like that."

As a roommate, Candace had been a dream come true—funny, tough, strong, smart—pretty much every good adjective you could think of. One of my only complaints about her was that she was always so definitive about everything she said, whether she knew what she was talking about or not. Candace believed there was no greater sin in this world than being wishy-washy.

"No," she said again. "She was back at school, setting up her new room, right? It's after midnight. She tells Karen Braverhoff—"

Her roommate.

"—that she's going down to the all-night deli to buy some snacks—"

"What snacks?"

Candace sighed. She always complained that I asked lots of dumb questions. It was true. When I was scared—which was pretty much all the time—I tried to focus on tiny details.

"A pint of ice cream for herself," Candace said, "and a Yoo-Hoo for Karen. *Okay?* The point is, she never came back."

"Oh," I said. I had to admit, this sounded bad. Barnard was smack in the middle of a not-so-great neighborhood in crime-infested murder-plagued New York City. Every time you left your dorm, especially at night, you were stepping knee-deep into a shark pool. There was this incredible electricity about New York; part of the thrill came from knowing you could get shot at any second. These past few years stray shootings had been felling victims while they sat *indoors*—reading a book, watching TV, diapering a baby. And now someone I knew had stepped outside and hadn't been heard from again.

"She didn't even take her wallet," Candace said.

3

"Why? How could she pay for the food without her wallet? That sounds screwy."

"Karen told the cops that all she took was a five dollar bill crumpled up in her hand."

"Why?"

"Because she was wearing leggings and didn't have any pockets. The point is—"

"Wait a minute, wait a minute," I said, trying to sort it all out. "Why did her mom call you now? It's three days later. She just started to get panicked now?"

"No, no, no, no. The cops have been on the case since Tuesday night."

The night Jenny disappeared.

"They have?" I puzzled over this. I'd been reading up on criminology this summer, and so I knew this wasn't standard practice. "But I thought with a missing person they had to wait for at least—"

"Not in Manhattan, okay? Not in a case like this. There are those two other girls that are still missing, remember?"

I could never forget. Before Candace and I had ever set foot on campus, two Barnard girls—Lauren Leiter and Melita Sanchez—had disappeared into the night much the way Jenny had. Lauren had vanished six years ago, Melita two years ago. You still saw flyers with their pictures on all the bulletin boards and bus kiosks around school. When our dorm counselors wanted to remind us to be careful and take all the standard security precautions, all they had to do was say Leiter and Sanchez and our hearts would freeze.

Once, freshman year, the girls' parents had come through the dorms, trying to meet everyone personally. The four parents had these nervous looks plastered

4

on their faces as they desperately sought new information. They were obviously trying to cling to their last shred of hope. It was awful.

Then, in April, the *Columbia Spectator* had run an editorial on the murders titled "Why Can't These Cases Be Solved?" The article was very critical of the police and FBI. A spokesperson for the FBI admitted that they hadn't made much progress on either girl's disappearance, and said that in both cases the trail of clues had gone cold. The FBI refused to comment on the question of a possible link between the Leiter and Sanchez disappearances.

I had read enough newspapers and followed enough political scandals to know that in America, *no comment* meant *yes*. I clipped the editorial for my writing file. It had started the wheels turning.

"So why didn't she call you before now?" I asked.

"She didn't call me before now because she didn't know to call me," Candace explained. "She's been going through all the stuff in Jenny's room trying to find some hint or clue about where she could have gone and she finally found her address book about an hour ago."

"Ah. Where was it?" I asked.

"Where was what?"

"The address book."

Another sigh.

"What's the difference?" Candace asked.

"I don't know, just tell me."

"You're nuts, you know that?"

"I agree. Now tell me."

"It was in the back pocket of a pair of jeans at the bottom of Jenny's laundry bag. Now Mrs. Silver's calling every name in there trying to see if anyone—"

My other line beeped.

"Uh-oh," I said.

"That's probably her. Listen, be extra nice to her, Ellie, because she sounds like she's about to fall into a million p—"

"Hold on."

I reached toward my bedside table and fumbled in the dark for the phone's flash button. "Hello?"

"Ellie?"

I recognized the sad nasal voice of Abby Rovere.

Abby was this short plump girl whom I had met in my American lit. seminar first semester. Candace once said that the reason I was such good friends with Abby was that she was the only person I knew who was more depressed, neurotic, and fearful than I. In a way she was right. But there was no way I was going to give up Abby. Most of my friends at school were friends of Candace's that I sort of tagged along with. Abby was *mine*.

"Hey, Abby!" I said happily. But then I felt guilty right away, like I had just laughed at Jenny's funeral or something.

"I am so sorry to call you so late," Abby said, "but I just got this really upsetting call and I—"

"About Jenny Silver, I know."

"You know?"

"Yeah. It's awful, isn't it?"

"Did her mom call you, too?" She sounded a little disappointed that I had spoiled her surprise.

"No. Candace called. She's on the other line. Can I call you right back?"

There was a silence. Abby was jealous of my close friendship and roommateship with Candace, I knew.

6

"Sure," she said. "You don't even have to call back, I just wanted to make sure you heard the news."

"Abby, don't be like that, of course I'm going to call you back. And how was your summer, by the way?"

"Horrible."

"Not as bad as mine, I'm sure."

"Worse."

I laughed. "You haven't heard how bad mine was yet."

"I guarantee mine was worse."

"I can't wait to hear," I said, which was true. During dark nights of the soul, Abby's sadsack tales were one of the few things I could count on to cheer me up.

I reached for the flash button. "Well, I better get back to—"

"God, it's so horrible, isn't it?" asked Abby. "I mean, you don't think anything really bad could have happened to Jenny, do you?"

I'm a very pessimistic person. I expect bad things to happen every second. If Jenny was missing, I assumed she was dead.

"I don't know," I said. "I hope not."

"Oh, wow, this is really the last thing I needed. That sounds selfish, I know, but it's true, I didn't need—"

"Abby? I better call you back."

"Oh, yeah, okay, sorry, you know I completely forgot about you being on the other line? I mean, I am just so upset. Mrs. Silver was crying hysterically and—"

"I'll call you right back."

"Call me tomorrow," Abby said. "After Mrs. Silver

7

called, I got so worked up I had to take a Valium. I think I may be asleep already, I'm not even sure."

"I *thought* you sounded pretty calm, considering the news."

I told Abby I would call her tomorrow night after I was moved into my new apartment. Then I pressed the flash button again. "Candace? You still there?"

"If I could get my hands on the creep that did this to her, whatever they did to her, I would rip his throat out, you know that?"

"Yeah," I said.

Candace was the campus leader of the Barnard Girls Take Back the Night movement and had led several midnight marches against neighborhood crime. She was a New Yorker through and through. If a cab turned too sharply into a crosswalk while she was headed across the street, she'd pound on the hood and shout out obscenities. Candace wasn't one to shy away from a fight. If she got a hold of Jenny's attacker, I had no doubt that the attacker would be toast.

"Was that her mom?" she asked.

"No. Abby."

"Oh, thanks a lot. You kept me waiting all that time and it wasn't even her mom?"

"Sorry."

Candace laughed. With all her confidence, she wasn't sensitive to slights. Unlike Abby, or my mother. With Candace, you didn't have to walk on eggshells.

"Just disappeared," she said as if to herself. "I can't get my mind around this."

"Maybe we should think about exactly what might have happened," I said. "You know, try to brainstorm it."

Candace swore.

8

"Uh, like, let's see," I said, "maybe she was kidnapped."

As soon as I said the word *kidnapped,* I shivered violently. There was a case a few years back where some criminals kidnapped the chairman of some big company and buried him in a deep hole in Riverside Park for two weeks while they tried to extort money from the family. Somehow the man had survived the ordeal. He was hailed as a big hero. The case gave me nightmares for weeks. I have every fear and phobia known to Man. I can walk into a drugstore and feel the symptoms for anything I see the treatment for. But being buried alive, that was right up there on my top-ten list of all-time terrors.

"Kidnapped?" Candace said. "I don't know. Maybe."

Not a word Candace used too often.

"Probably not," she added.

That was more like her.

"Definitely not," she concluded. "It's been three days. If she was kidnapped, they would have contacted the parents by now, asking for the ransom money."

"Yeah, you're probably right."

Another possibility occurred to me.

"What if while she was walking to the store—"

"She bought the ice cream."

"What?"

"The grocers remembered her. They told the cops she bought the ice cream."

"What kind?"

"Ellie."

"Just tell me."

"Ben and Jerry's."

"Flavor?"

She spat out the answer. "Cherry Garcia. Anyway, that means she was walking *back* from the store. We know that much. Which gives us about two blocks to play with. Somewhere two blocks from campus . . . unbelievable."

"Okay," I said, "so what if while she's walking back from the store with the ice cream in her hand, she runs into that guy she's so crazy about. The one she started dating during finals. What's his name?"

"Stuart Englander."

"Stuart, right."

I'd never met Stuart, but I'd heard about him. He was supposed to be this tall studly junior from L.A.

"So Stuart is with some friends," I said, "and they just got back to school and now they're going off for one last wild trip to the woods or something before settling down to the grind. And they've got a car and they see Jenny walking down Broadway with a pint of Cherry Garcia. 'Hey, Jenny!' they call to her. 'Hop in!' So Jenny hops in and disappears. Tomorrow she'll be back all sunburned and saying she's sorry for making us worry."

"Stuart's still in California."

"He is? How do you know?"

"Ellie, take my word for it."

"How do you know?"

From the length of the pause, Candace must have counted to ten. "He's rooming with Grady this year, okay?"

Grady Justice was her ex-boyfriend and now-friend.

"Oh. Then what if—"

"Ellie," Candace said, "she's dead."

"Dead? What are you talking about? We don't know that."

"I know it."

Even though I was assuming the same thing, I shuddered.

"How do you know?"

"It's like, I can feel it," Candace said.

"Oh, come on, don't tell me you're suddenly into that psychic crap."

"I'm not, but it's like her presence is gone, you know?"

I started to sweat. Because I knew what Candace meant. It was as if the universe was missing something. The air was lighter. One soul had departed.

I pictured Jenny. She was tall. For some reason I couldn't picture her face at that moment. Then I remembered her dark and copious freckles, how it looked as if a taxi had driven by and splattered her face with tiny spots of mud. As soon as I pictured those freckles, I saw her whole face, smiling as always, a classic, all-American cheerleader of a girl.

"Dead," I repeated softly.

"But I'm going to find out who did it, I promise you that."

"Candace," I said, "that's a job for the police."

I wasn't worried that Candace would get herself into trouble. Coward that I am, I was worried she would drag *me* into trouble right along with her.

"The police!" Candace snarled. "Are you kidding? The police are a bunch of lazy and corrupt— I mean, look at those other two girls. Did they *ever* find them? No. They never even found their bodies."

She had a point.

"Please, Candace," I said, "don't tell me stuff like that. If I can't trust the police, I'll have a total nervous breakdown. Even in my nightmares I dream about dialing nine-one-one."

11

"Okay, but I'm telling you," Candace said, "the police are going to be useless on this. What do I always tell you, Ell? There's only one person you can trust. And that's yourself. And me, of course." She laughed.

"Okay," she said, "I'm getting off, I want to make some more calls. Maybe *I* can find someone who saw her. Call me if you hear anything, and vice versa. I mean it."

"Yeah."

"You all packed, by the way?"

Tomorrow morning Candace and Grady were driving a rented Ryder van out to my house in Englewood, New Jersey. We were going to load up my stuff, then swing around to her parents' loft in Greenwich Village to pick up Candace's stuff, then head up to our new two-bedroom off-campus apartment on West 112th Street.

"Pretty much all set," I said.

"Good. Jesus," she said, "this makes me mad. Jenny was a good kid, you know that? Was, listen to me. Is. Is. Is. Is!"

"Is," I agreed, trying to sound hopeful.

"Don't bother going to sleep, 'cause Mrs. Silver is going to wake you right up again, as soon as she works her way down to the Ss in Jenny's address book."

Candace was right. About twenty minutes later the phone rang again.

"H-hello. Is this Ellie Sommers?"

"Yes?"

"I am so sorry to wake you up like this—"

"You're not waking me up."

"—but it's a terrible emergency, I'm afraid . . . "

12

Sounds of crying.

"Uh, is this Mrs. Silver?"

There was a stunned pause. "Yes," she said tensely. "How did you know?"

"Mrs. Silver, I'm so sorry that your daughter is, uh, you know, missing, but I'm sure that she'll—"

"Have you heard from her? What have you heard? Have you talked to her? Where is she?"

"No, no, no, I haven't talked to her, but a friend of mine, Candace Burkett—you called her earlier? She already called me. Just to, uh, tell me the news."

There was a terrible silence as the hopes I had accidentally raised crashed back down to earth.

"So you don't know where she is?" Mrs. Silver asked.

"No, I'm afraid I don't."

"Oh, dear God."

"I'm so sorry." I winced. That sounded like Jenny was dead and I was offering my condolences. "Uh," I stammered, feeling red and fuzzy with embarrassment, "I didn't really know her all that well—" I rolled my eyes in horror, realizing I had used the past tense.

"No one's heard from her," her mother said hollowly. "No one."

There was an awful pause. I clutched the receiver helplessly; I couldn't think of a thing to say. Finally I said, "I was just saying to my friend, uh, Candace, that there are probably a million different explanations for where—"

My voice sounded horribly phony in my ears. Mrs. Silver interrupted. "If you hear anything, or think of anything at all that might help us find her, will you call this number?"

13

I wrote the number down. Then Mrs. Silver hung up so she could make her next call.

I lay in the dark, staring up at the dragon-shaped crack in the ceiling's white paint.

I could still hear the pain and fear in Mrs. Silver's voice.

Jenny's disappearance hadn't seemed real to me until just then.

Now it seemed real.

CHAPTER 2

I GOT OUT OF BED AND SAT DOWN AT MY desk. I was naked. My back and tush stuck to the leather cushions in a moist unpleasant kiss. My parents didn't have central air-conditioning, and my room had no air conditioner, which was one of the many things that had made mine a hellish summer. I had the windows in my room wide-open, but there seemed to be no air moving in or out. A few moths fluttered against the dark screens. Outside I could hear the faint crackly whine of the telephone lines and power cables; I had read an article somewhere that said you could get cancer from the radiation emitted by those power lines.

I opened the bottom drawer and pulled out a thick stack of paper.

The previous spring I had come up with an amazing plan. No trip across Europe, no glamorous summer internship for me. No, no, no. *I* would live at home with my depressed father and my even more depressed mother. I would write a screenplay, and I would sell it for a million dollars.

From the moment the plan occurred to me, I was deliriously happy. All my life I had loved movies. I'd watched so many of them, I figured how hard could it be to write one?

As soon as I hit on my plan, I started fantasizing about how great my sophomore year would be once I was famous. Oh, how modestly I would act, and how jealous all the other Barnard girls would be! And every guy at Columbia—Barnard's brother school—would fall all over himself to ask me out.

The idea for my screenplay came from that editorial in the *Spectator*. I asked myself, what if the two missing persons cases really were linked? I was going to call my screenplay *Stalker*. It would be about a serial killer who stalks the Barnard campus.

I spent the first weeks of summer reading books about the police, the FBI, and the search for serial killers. Then I wrote about forty pages of the screenplay. And *then*—

I realized I had no plot. I reread what I had written and got so depressed I didn't write another word. I just hung around the house or went to the movies by myself or called friends from school and was unable to reach them because they were all off having thrilling exciting summers.

That last night of the summer, after I talked to Mrs. Silver, was the first time I reopened the lower drawer of my desk.

I set the papers on my desk. Gaped at them.
Unbelievable.

I could feel the short hairs on the back of my neck standing up, feel the drops of sweat on my forehead evaporating and giving me a chill, even though there was no breeze.

16

What if . . .

What if all the time I had been trying to write my screenplay about a serial killer, the real drama had been writing itself?

What if . . . while I struggled with my made-up script, a real-live murderer was on the loose in Manhattan?

What if . . .

The killer had just claimed victim number three?

Even though I was up very late, I woke extra early. My mom was puttering around the kitchen when I came down for breakfast. She gave me the briefest of smiles, then went back to cleaning the counter with a sponge. I knew that smile. She was upset.

I gave her a little hug, earning another tiny smile for my trouble. Then I took out a box of Quaker Oats low-fat granola and a carton of skim milk and slumped into my regular kitchen chair.

"So," my mother said softly, "I heard your phone ringing last night."

"Oh?"

When my mother slept and when she ate were two of the world's great mysteries. For lunch she usually had a Ritz cracker with a dab of margarine and a handful of grapes. At night she always seemed to be up. Anything that happened in the house she commented on the next morning. By the way, Ellie, I heard you turning over in your bed at three last night; couldn't sleep?

"Yeah," I said, trying to sound ever so casual. "I got a late call."

As if that would end the discussion.

I was starting to feel very nervous. I hadn't even stopped to think what the news about Jenny was going to do to my poor mother.

"Who was it?" Mom asked.

"Uh, Candace."

"She called awfully late."

"That's Candace. I hope she didn't bother you."

"Oh, I was up, I was up." My mother gave me a searching look. "Everything okay?"

"Everything's fine." I grinned at her.

"Ellie! Not with your mouth full."

"Sorry."

I watched her scrubbing the brass handles on the cupboard door. It killed me.

Candace was always telling me that I was very attractive (or would be if I would just stop slouching). She said that guys were always asking her about me (but for some strange reason they were never asking *me* about me). Despite what Candace said, when I looked in the mirror, I saw only faults and flaws. I was tall. I saw myself as gangly, goofy.

I got that from Dad. Also from my dad I inherited a slightly droopy nose—like it was melting and there was a droplet of flesh gathering at the tip.

Mom, on the other hand, had this petite fragile beauty that always made her seem Japanese to me, like she should have been wearing a beautiful dark print kimono. But the look she usually had on her face suggested she was in terrible pain, which I guess she was.

To name one of her many problems, Mom felt she was a worthless failure. She had never figured out what she wanted to do with her life. Even her fine

18

looks didn't please her. My father was a math professor, first at Columbia, then Princeton. Mom was always jealous of Dad's young female students, always talking about how pretty they were, always saying how they were prettier than she was.

She'd been taking lithium for years to help her with her depression and anxiety. Recently she'd switched to the new antidepressant of choice, Prozac. I didn't see that it was helping.

"Mom," I said. "The kitchen is spotless. Please— why don't you just relax?"

"Relax," she said, scoffing, as if the notion itself were ridiculous.

"Why not?" I asked.

"Because there's way too much to do," she said. "This is a very big house, you know."

"I know," I said. She started wiping down the countertop. "Hey, I've got an idea. Since you hate to see me go to school so much, why don't you take another course at Columbia so we can be together?"

Six years ago my mother had taken an art-history class as part of Columbia's general-studies program, which offered classes to anyone with a college degree. It had been my father's idea. He was teaching at Columbia at the time, so Mom could commute to the city with him twice a week. Maybe even get a second degree in something.

She had taken only one course, found the pressure of the course work too much for her, and dropped out midsemester. She had tried again two years later, taking Abnormal Psych. (which was right up her alley, believe me), but had dropped that class as well after only a couple of weeks.

"So when is Candace coming?" she asked.

19

The way she asked, it was like a prisoner asking, "How long till my execution?"

"Couple of hours."

She sighed.

"Mom," I said, "I'll be fine." But what I was thinking was, Jenny Silver was not fine. And if my mom found out, she'd break in two.

"So crazy," she murmured.

"What is?"

"Going there."

"Where?"

"Barnard."

"Why? It's one of the top schools in the country."

"You know what I mean."

I did. We'd had this same discussion a hundred times.

"Mom," I said, "you're so worried about me living in Manhattan, meanwhile while I was at school last year, you got robbed."

They had been at an all-Brahms concert by the New Jersey Symphony. When they came back, Mom stepped on an earring in the living room. At least the robbery was a professional job; the burglar, or burglars, had come while my parents were out and had skillfully disabled a five-thousand-dollar alarm system. It could have been a lot worse. Still, it was terrifying.

"If you're trying to claim that Englewood, New Jersey, is more dangerous than New York City . . ." Mom said, waving her sponge at me.

I heard footsteps down the front steps. Then the front door opened and closed. Then my father came in. His silver hair was still mussed from sleep. He was wearing his tattered old blue bathrobe (though my parents had always been reasonably comfortable money-wise, neither one believed in buying anything new). He was carrying the morning's *New York Times,* which he read every morning as religiously as my mother cleaned.

He gave Mom a kiss, me a smile, and patted my cheek. Then he tossed the paper on the table next to his place setting and sat down. Immediately my mother busied herself serving him his breakfast, pouring his OJ and coffee, shaking out his heart medication, two red-and-yellow capsules.

"Mom," I said, "let him get his own breakfast. He's a big boy."

She shot me a look.

I don't know why I bothered trying to change her. She had been this way my whole life, waiting on my father hand and foot. This was my last day at home, I should have given her a break. But I couldn't.

"You didn't serve *me* my breakfast, I noticed."

She rolled her eyes.

"So," Dad said to me as he unfolded his paper napkin on his lap, "today's the big day, huh? Nervous?"

"No." At least, I wasn't nervous about school.

He looked surprised. "Good."

And then I saw it. At the bottom of the front page was a photo of a smiling teenage girl with bangs and freckles. Jenny Silver. With the headline, BARNARD GIRL MISSING.

Sometimes in New York City there were several murders in a single night. The news would be reported in tiny items in the middle of the *Times* B-section. But a rich girl from an Ivy League school . . .

"Can I see this a sec?" I asked, reaching for the paper.

21

My father looked amazed. It was a hard-and-fast house rule. No one touched Daddy's paper until he was done reading it. You couldn't even read the sports section until he had read the whole thing. He didn't like a messy paper. But now I pulled off the front section.

"I have to go to the bathroom," I announced, faking a yawn. I tucked the paper under my arm and started toward the door.

Both my parents were staring at me very strangely.

"What is it?" my mother said.

"What is what?"

My mother might have been crazy, but she wasn't dumb. "What's in the paper?" she asked.

No one ever will ever have to give me a lie-detector test. All you have to do is ask me a direct question, then squint at me with a worried look, and I'll confess to anything. Right now I had this gigantic grin on my face. I was going to lie, but I could tell there was no point. "You're only going to get upset," I said.

I dropped the paper back on the table. My mother hurried over. She read the article over my father's shoulder. Then she looked up at me. She looked so wounded, it was scary. I felt as guilty at that moment as if I was responsible for Jenny's disappearance myself.

"Oh my God," Mom said. "Did you know this girl?"

"A little."

"Oh my God."

"Oh dear," my father said. "Oh dear."

This was my parents in a nutshell—oh my God and oh dear.

"That's why Candace called?" my mother asked.

I nodded.

22

This revelation only seemed to add to my mother's sense of horror. She put a hand over her mouth and sat down slowly, her head turned from both me and Dad.

"Marcia," Dad said gently. She didn't turn to look at him.

"Mom," I said. "I've told you a hundred times. New York City is a gigantic place. You sit here and you read about all the bad stuff happening there, and you feel like it's so dangerous. But you've got to remember the statistics." The statistics were horrible, but I wasn't going to bring that up. "The odds of anything happening are teensy weensy."

This was a paraphrase of Dad's standard speech that he used to try to calm Mom down about the dangers I was facing. You could tell it was Dad's speech because of the emphasis on numbers and statistics, which was Dad's version of going to the movies way too much. It was his way of disconnecting from the world.

The statistics argument never worked on Mom when Dad used it, and it never worked when I used it, but we tried it anyway.

"Isn't that right?" I said to Dad.

"That's exactly right," he said.

My mother didn't say a word.

"Mom, I studied statistics last year, remember? I know what I'm talking about. People's fears are irrational. Like some guy is deathly afraid of flying, but at the same time he's driving around without a seat belt, which is a hundred times more dangerous."

I saw Dad's eyebrows go up. He managed to resist correcting my figures.

"Statistics," Mom said, spitting out the word.

We waited.

"Well," she said finally. "You're not going back, that's all. It would be insane to go."

"Mom—" I said.

"Marcia," said Dad, "she has to go to school."

"But not that school! Girls just disappearing off the streets."

"What girls?" Dad said. "This is one girl. One single instance."

Not true, but I wasn't going to enlighten them.

Mom slapped the table with her hand. "Not going!" she cried.

I'm not a brave person. I probably would have done exactly what Mom advised—if she hadn't insisted on it. But the way she kept begging me and ordering me and pleading with me, I felt like if I didn't go back to school now, I'd never leave. Maybe I'd never leave the house, just sit in my room till I was ninety. So instead of staying home or transferring schools, I ended up acting a lot more courageous than I felt. I said I was going back to Barnard no matter what.

Mom began to sob and rushed up to her bedroom. Dad hurried after her. And I sat in the kitchen by myself, feeling exhausted and very afraid.

When Candace arrived, I met her at the front door. I almost didn't recognize her. She was tanned almost to burned from a recent white-water rafting trip. And she had gotten her auburn hair cut really short like a boy; the haircut made her large green eyes look bigger and braver than ever. She gave me a big hug. I felt like I was getting my batteries recharged, the hug felt so good. It was like I was being rescued, rescued from the House of Gloom.

Grady was leaning against the Ryder van in the driveway, looking handsome and appealing in a blue button-down shirt and khaki pants. As always, he was polishing his wire-frame glasses. He looked up and waved.

And right then, after the long dreary summer, I felt such an intense surge of excitement at seeing my old friends. . . .

Nothing could go wrong, nothing could harm me, I told myself, as long as I was around Candace and her crowd.

Which, looking back on it, was one of the stupidest things I've ever told myself.

CHAPTER 3

MOM DIDN'T COME OUT OF HER BEDROOM again until Candace, Grady, my father, and I had finished loading the van with all my stuff. First Mom opened her bedroom window to shout down at Dad not to hurt his back. Then she came out to the van to say good-bye.

Candace was at the wheel. Grady was sitting next to her, polishing his glasses again. I was by the passenger-side window. Which was where my mom's gaunt face appeared, eyes rimmed red from crying.

"I don't want you to go," she said quietly.

"I know that," I said.

"I think it's a mistake. A big one."

"I know. But it's not. It's the right thing to do. I'll be fine. Right, guys?"

"Right," Grady and Candace agreed.

I introduced Grady, whom Mom hadn't met before. "You two should get together," I said. "Grady is actually neater than you are. He likes to spend hours with a roll of Scotch tape getting lint off his clothes and—"

"Sweetheart," Mom said softly. "Will you promise me something?"

"Sure."

"Will you promise me . . . you'll be very . . ."

She started crying again before she could say the word *careful*.

"Candace," I said, "will you tell my mom how safe our building is?"

"It's totally safe. Well, not totally, you know, because nothing is totally safe—"

"Candace," I said.

"It's very safe," Grady said; he really didn't know what he was talking about, but I appreciated the comment anyway.

"Mrs. Sommers," he went on in his slight southern drawl, "I'm from Charleston, ma'am, so I know how you feel. I used to be terrified of the Big Apple myself. Believe me, it's not nearly so bad as you think it is." He blew on his glasses and started in again, rubbing them with yet another lens wipe. "You're out here and you're reading news reports. You forget that it's a huge city and . . ."

Basically it was the statistics speech all over again.

Grady was twenty and a Columbia senior, one of a string of boyfriends that Candace had had and discarded freshman year while I burned with jealousy. He had this soft-featured face and light blond hair, the kind of hair that's so light it looks a little albino-ish. But he had these baby-blue eyes that made the whole face work like gangbusters. And his southern-gentleman charm and his soothing voice were coming in awfully handy right now as he worked at calming my mother.

"But to live off-campus," my mother kept saying, shaking her head as if trying to wake from a bad dream.

27

"Mrs. Sommers?" Candace said, leaning past Grady. "Did Ellie tell you about old Molly?"

"I told her," I said.

Candace went on anyway. "She's the super. She's this amazing woman. A real fireball. And all she cares about in life is protecting Barnard girls. I'm serious. Half the time she's out front sweeping with this old broom, watching over her place. She says we're all her children. That's how she thinks of us. She knows everything that goes on in her building. Everyone who goes in or out, she looks them over. If it's a guy, she practically arrests them. She interrogates them before they can go inside."

"So there's no doorman?" Mom said, sniffing.

"Old Molly is better than having a doorman," Candace said. "You know, a doorman isn't a security guard. His job is to open the door. There have been thousands of people mugged in Manhattan in doorman buildings."

"Not thousands," I said, giving Candace a horrified look.

"Okay," Candace said, "just a few. Whatever. The point is, what's the doorman going to do if someone comes in with a gun or a knife? Now get this, old Molly has been the super in the building for six years. And in six years there hasn't been a single break-in or robbery or mugging. Not one. You can call the New York Police Department and they'll tell you it's true. That's why people are just dying to get into that building."

Dying. Great choice of words. Mom looked twice as scared as before Candace got started calming her down.

"It's safer than a dorm," Candace concluded. "Really."

Dad had an arm around Mom, half holding her up. "Maybe you just better go," he told us.

"Shouldn't Grady drive?" Mom asked.

Candace grinned. Some things made her so mad she had to smile. People assuming that men were better than women at anything—including weight lifting—gave Candace instant heartburn.

"Candace is an excellent driver, Mom," I said quickly.

"Much better than I am," Grady chimed in.

"Last summer she drove cross-country," I added.

"Okay," my mother said. She tried to smile. Then she leaned into the car to kiss me good-bye.

I had been feeling embarrassed for my mother—and even more for me—the way she'd been crying like this in front of my friends. But when she kissed me, I started crying, too.

"Okay?" Candace said, her green eyes glittering. She was still angry, I could tell. "We all set?"

"Uh-huh," I said, blubbering.

"Call us tonight," Dad told me.

"Call on the way," Mom said through her tears.

"Maybe I should just stay home," I said suddenly.

"Oh, for God's sake," Candace said. She put the van in reverse and backed out of the driveway so sharply that she nicked the mailbox. A good way to set my mother's heart at ease about her driving skills.

As we pulled out I saw my father waving to me, still holding Mom; she had buried her face against his chest. She looked so tiny. I was sobbing.

"I'm sorry," I told my friends through my tears.

"That's okay," Grady said softly. "It's good to have feelings. Shows you're alive."

When he said that, I wanted to bury my head

against his chest. Mom was lucky, I told myself self-pityingly. At least she had a shoulder to cry on. I wiped my nose with the back of my arm.

"I know she's not the happiest woman in the world," Candace said as she braked for a stop sign. "And I don't want to say anything bad about her. . . ."

"Then don't," I said.

"Don't," Grady agreed.

"But that crack about my driving," Candace said.

To her credit, she didn't say anything more.

"You were really doing a wonderful job of making her feel secure, by the way," I told Candace. "Knives and guns—thanks a lot."

Candace looked at me and laughed. "Sorry. You're right. Sometimes I'm an idiot. It's rare, but it happens."

What I was thinking was, Turn back. That's what I wanted to shout. Turn back, Candace, and take me home where life may be incredibly depressing, but at least it's safe.

But I didn't say anything.

I let Candace drive us closer and closer to New York.

CHAPTER 4

JUST TO SHOW YOU THE TOTAL TRUST I HAD in Candace, I hadn't set foot inside our new apartment. Last April two upperclass friends of hers had told her she could sublet the place if she wanted, since they were graduating and had two years left on their lease. She told me the apartment was great, and that was good enough for me. I wrote out a check for my half of the security deposit and left it at that.

I had seen the outside of the building, though. And even though Candace said that this nutty old woman, Molly, was always out front, she wasn't out front last semester when I went to stare at the building's dirty brick facade. Nor was she out front this evening at around five when we finally pulled up with our belongings stuffed in the back of the van.

There were so many cars double-parked on the narrow street that Candace had to park in front of a hydrant across from our building. We all got out of the cab of the truck and stretched. We stared across the street at our new home.

Two-fifty-one West 112th Street was a short

brownstone that was sandwiched so tightly between two tall buildings it looked as if it had been squeezed thin. Even though it was tiny, the building had an awning, which gave the whole place the shape of a boot.

I told this to Grady, who told me I was very creative and going to be a famous writer someday. So after that I always called the building the Boot.

Candace clapped. "Okay, we better get started 'cause we have to return the van before seven or we get charged for a whole other day. Uh, Ellie, why don't you wait by the van for the first shift and make sure we don't get a ticket and Grady and I will start unloading."

I frowned.

"Stuart will be around any minute," Candace promised, "and he'll relieve you."

"Stuart? Stuart Englander?"

"He's my new roommate," Grady said. The way he frowned when he said this suggested to me that there was already trouble in paradise.

I watched as Candace and Grady piled their arms with boxes and bags and started across the wide street, Candace in the lead. Candace crossed the street the way she always crossed Manhattan streets. She just crossed. Traffic or no traffic. Let them stop, that was her philosophy. Usually, when I crossed with her, Candace would make it to the other side and stand there waving at me impatiently to come on, while I would end up getting trapped in the middle of the road with taxis and buses and cars whooshing by on either side of me, coming terrifyingly close to hitting me, too; I'd just stand there with my eyes closed, feeling totally helpless, waiting for the stampede to pass me by.

There was a lot of honking, but Candace and Grady made it safely across. I watched them approach the building. Candace set down the boxes she was carrying, found her keys, went inside, and unlocked the inner door. She held the door open for Grady, who wedged it with my box of film books and screenplays. Then Candace retrieved her load, and then they both disappeared into the darkness.

I leaned against the van. It was five o'clock but still sunny. Even though I was scared about Jenny, it felt great to be back in Manhattan. I watched the people walking down the street. A Chinese student I only vaguely recognized strolled by with a big pile of books under his arm. I waved at him; he gave me a puzzled look. Then came an old homeless woman whom I had given change to on more than one occasion. She stopped to rifle through a trash can for refundable soda bottles. I felt like waving hello to her as well, but restrained myself.

And then a tall handsome guy with curly black hair and tanned skin started loping down the street toward me. He was wearing a ripped T-shirt and a faded pair of blue Columbia shorts and unlaced sockless sneakers. A slob, but good-looking enough that it didn't matter, which he seemed to know. He waved at *me*.

I waved back.

When he came close, he looked surprised. "You're not Candace, are you?"

"No."

"Ellie? The roommate?"

"Yeah."

"Thought so."

What was *that* supposed to mean?

"Stuart Englander." He stood there grinning at me,

33

hands on his hips, as if I should have fainted with excitement just to be in his presence.

"Oh, Stuart, yeah, hi."

He was even better close up. He had this strong jaw and a dimple in his chin and was basically a hunk. Even though I was immediately repulsed by the ego of the guy—which came off him in waves—I immediately fantasized about being married to him. I'd write my million-dollar screenplay while he hovered in the background looking cute and bringing me toasted bagels and orange juice that he'd squeeze himself. . . .

"So," Stuart said, gazing across the street, "where's this famous Candace that my roommate has been writing to me about all summer?"

Thus shattered another sweet fantasy. That's what every guy wanted to know from me. Where was Candace?

"She and Grady took the first load inside."

"Ah."

He looked instantly bored.

"Pretty awful about Jenny, huh?" I asked. For one thing, I wanted to make conversation, even if it meant using poor Jenny to do it. For another, I wanted to make Stuart feel bad for acting so nonchalant when a girl he had dated was missing.

Didn't seem to work.

"Yeah, lousy," he agreed. "I saw her just last week, the day she got back. She was all excited about the new semester and switching her major to American studies and—well, I hope she's okay."

Something was bothering me. "You saw her last week? I thought you were in L.A."

"What?" He frowned at me, reddening through his

34

California tan. "Did I say I saw her? No, no, I talked to her on the phone is what I meant." He squinted at me as if it had just come to his attention that I existed. "What's your major, by the way?"

The eternal college question. I had once spent an hour trying to think of witty replies.

My major? Dog farts. What's yours?

My major? Major Strasser in Casablanca, *which is also my favorite movie. What's yours?*

As you can see, I hadn't come up with anything good, and so I always answered with the truth. "English and a minor in creative writing."

"Oh, yeah, you write? So do I."

He was gazing across the street at the Boot, not even looking at me as he said this. It was clear he wasn't interested in what I wrote—nor did he believe that I was a real writer. Unlike him, I'm sure. I certainly wasn't going to ask him what kinds of stuff *he* wrote. I decided to let the topic drop for all eternity.

"Well, I guess I better get started unloading this crap," he said.

"Yeah," I said. "Nice to meet you."

I watched as he took three boxes of books, probably herniating himself in an effort to impress my stunning roommate, and staggered across the street.

It was a pretty easy move, as moves go. The hardest part was watching Stuart and Grady falling all over themselves as they tried to impress Candace and ignored me altogether. The second hardest part was Candace's red brocade sofa. It was a four-person job. We left the van by the hydrant and just hoped we didn't get a ticket.

The stairs of the brownstone were narrow. We had to tilt the sofa through a whole series of odd angles to

35

work it up to the fourth floor. When we finally got the thing inside, Candace collapsed on it, so of course Grady and Stuart collapsed on it as well. They were all laughing hysterically. I staggered into the kitchen, pulled a dirty glass out of the cupboard, filled it with warm water from the cold-water tap, and guzzled it down. I thought my back was broken. I could already hear my parents shouting "I told you so!" as they visited me in the hospital where I lay in traction. I was drenched with sweat, too, which was embarrassing in front of two guys.

We were almost done unloading the van, just a couple of lamps and a wicker wastebasket. Rather than watch the guys wooing Candace, I went out to get the lamps. When I came back inside, Candace and Grady were leaving to return the van, and when I got upstairs Stuart rushed off (to the gym, he said) as if he were terrified of being alone with me for a second.

I sat on the sofa, staring at the apartment. It was shabby and needed a paint job, but it had definite potential and charm—a curved archway led from the living room to a hallway that led either way to the bedrooms. It was a prewar building and the apartment had high ceilings and nice moldings.

On the other hand, the floors were curved and rickety. The cupboards in the kitchen were made of old creaky wood that stuck horribly and had to be yanked open every time. And then I looked in the lone bathroom. The toilet was tilted, actually tilted, the Leaning Tower of Toilet.

But still, the place was large, especially if you counted the long slashing entrance hallway as part of the floor space.

All in all it was the kind of apartment that anyone

36

outside of Manhattan would call a trash heap and anyone inside Manhattan would say "What a steal!" Especially for $830 a month.

Right now the apartment was deathly silent. Everything was in boxes. There was nothing on the walls. I was sure it would look great when we had everything set up. But at this moment it was incredibly depressing. I hurried downstairs. I went straight to the Hot Bagels store around the corner. But even two everything bagels with cream cheese and a cup of decaf couldn't cheer me up.

I was feeling lonely. I was also feeling scared.

The Barnard campus is tiny, especially compared with Columbia's huge campus right across the street. But there's a fortresslike effect. You go past a security guard and through a gate and you're in, you're safe. Instead, now I was living *off-campus*. It didn't take the rantings of my overprotective mother to convince me that this year would be riskier, and scarier.

And that was before Jenny had disappeared.

Yet here I was, right off the bat, doing the thing that scared me most about living off-campus, the thing that had given me restless nights all summer.

I was walking back to my apartment all by myself.

At night.

And just like Jenny, I was walking alone.

CHAPTER 5

SO I WAS WONDERFULLY RELIEVED WHEN I came back to the building and there was this big old woman out front under the awning, sweeping away.

"Molly?" I asked.

She stopped sweeping, eyed me. "Do I know you?"

"Not yet."

She grinned. "That's a relief. Because otherwise my mind is going. I never forget a face. Or at least that's what I like to tell myself. Ha-ha."

I laughed, too. Candace was right. I did like her. "I'm Eleanor Sommers, the new tenant in 4-B, with Candace Burkett?"

"Oh, yeah. Candace. I love that girl. She's a tiger," Molly growled. "She's fierce."

I nodded proudly. "Yup."

"I like that. I'm fierce, too." The big old woman hefted her broom like a weapon and made a sound like a samurai warrior. I laughed.

"You go to Barnard, too?" she asked me.

"Uh-huh."

"What year? Sophomore?"

"How did you know that?"

"Because of Candace. I remember she's a sopho-more, so I just figured. See, I'm pretty sharp even for an old biddy." She tapped the side of her big head. "I remembered."

"Not bad." I smiled. I did feel safer knowing this old woman was going to be watching over me. She was big, broad-shouldered, with a mass of scraggly white hair. She looked like she could tackle an intruder, if need be.

She glanced at her watch, then went back to sweeping. "So many children," she said, shaking her head.

"What's that?"

"You're all my children, you Barnard girls. Old Molly has to protect you. I got so many children, though, I don't know what to do. You have a boyfriend?"

"No."

"That's good."

I laughed again. "Why is that good? I was thinking maybe I should get some plastic surgery."

"No, it's good not to have a boyfriend. Men are evil."

"Oh, now."

"They are."

"I believe you, but I wouldn't know, they pretty much ignore me." More self-pity, I know. Self-pity cheers me up about as effectively as fattening bagels with cream cheese, but I couldn't help it.

Molly had gone back to sweeping.

"I take it *you* don't have a boyfriend?" I asked.

"Who me? No way. Old woman like me."

"You don't look old."

"I'm ancient. Anyway. I had a boyfriend. Sometimes he comes around. I tell him to leave me alone, but sometimes he comes around. He's no good."

"What's wrong with him?"

She made a tippling motion with her hand to show me that her friend drank.

"Ah."

"Listen, let me tell you some rules here. I don't like you girls to have boys over," she said. "Remember that. I'm strict about that."

"Well, don't worry about me. I've been following that rule religiously."

If she got the joke, she didn't smile.

"Did you hear about the Barnard girl who's missing?" I asked.

Molly's face darkened. "Horrible." She pointed the broom at me. "That's what I keep telling you girls, you've got to be careful. I try to take care of you, but you've got to help me. You've got to watch your back."

"I know."

"Really, you've got to be extra careful," she said.

I was getting scared all over again. "Right," I said.

Suddenly I didn't want to go into the dark building all by myself. Stalling, I watched Molly sweep.

"You're like my mother," I told her. "You keep cleaning even when it's spotless."

She smiled, showing a mouthful of rotten, crooked, and yellowed teeth. "Keeps me busy," she said. Then she glanced around as if there might be spies eavesdropping on our conversation and added, "I like to keep a watch on the building. I know everything that

40

goes on on this street, let me tell you. Try to keep my nose to the ground, see what I can pick up. We'll see. Maybe I can figure out what happened to that girl."

I nodded.

She studied me, then grinned. "You're a good girl," she said.

"I am?"

"You are. I can feel it." She tapped her chest. "Here."

"Thanks," I said.

She held out one big hand to shake, but when I took it she pulled me close for a big smothering and embarrassing hug. "There," she said, holding me at arm's length again. "Now you're welcomed into the building. Now you're Molly's friend."

It felt awkward, but I still appreciated the blessing. "Thanks."

She smiled at me.

"Well," I said, starting toward the door. "I guess I better . . ."

Molly nodded. "I'm in the basement if you need anything. Anything at all. Anytime day or night. I'm serious about that. Ask the other girls."

The Boot was one of those off-campus buildings that had become something of an informal dorm, so many Barnard girls had rented here and passed on their leases to other Barnard girls.

"That's great," I said.

"You ask Candace. She's had my chicken broth. Best chicken broth in the world."

"I can't wait."

I waved at her, as a way of trying to end the conversation formally. But as I fumbled with my new keys, trying to remember which one opened the downstairs lock, I thought I could feel Molly watching me.

I glanced back.

I think I was expecting the old woman to have turned into a grinning gargoyle. But she was just smiling warmly.

"Be good now," she said.

CHAPTER 6

THAT NIGHT CANDACE AND I UNPACKED AND set up the apartment. Which would have been fun, except Candace was on the cordless phone the whole time, making about a gazillion calls. Or she was down the hall with the Barnard girls who lived in 4-A, Jocelyn and Carmen. You would have thought Candace couldn't get anything done that way, making calls and socializing. But by the end of the evening, she hadn't just unpacked, she had already set up a group called Find Jenny. The group was going to meet once a week in our apartment.

Secretly I wanted to set up a group called Forget Jenny and Try to Pretend That Everything Is Okay and We Are Totally Safe.

I did get two calls of my own. Abby and Mom. But during both calls there was such a deluge of beeps from call waiting that I didn't try to talk to either of them for long.

Finally, after ten, Candace hung up the phone and said, "We have to go down to the police station right now."

"Now?"

She smiled. "Gotcha. No, tomorrow at three. They're interviewing everyone who knew—knows Jenny. You know, trying to see if they can find anything."

I didn't want to go to the police station. I didn't want to go anywhere near the police station. I wanted to bury my head in the sand. Candace must have read the look on my face because she said, "You're going."

When I woke up the next morning, those two words were still ringing in my head.

You're going.

Candace was already gone. Probably running a marathon. There was a note for me scrawled on the memo pad on the fridge.

Find Jenny! Our first meeting is this morning at
eleven. Place: Right here where you're standing!
Hope you can come.
Love ya,
C

Okay, I told myself. I'll pretend I didn't see the note. It was my first day back at school, after all. I figured I deserved a little R&R.

Especially since it was Sunday. Classes didn't start till tomorrow. I could take it easy. So what I did was, I put up my movie posters, then went out and bought the fat Sunday *Times*. I sat in the Hungarian Pastry Shop (one of the big local hangouts, where you could have a Danish and sit all day and the waitresses didn't bug you). I drank an espresso and got nowhere with the crossword puzzle even though the theme was

Oscar winners, which I thought I knew cold. Then I went over the Barnard course catalog and put check marks next to half the classes.

But . . .

I'm such a nervous person. I can't handle any kind of suspense. For one thing I was skipping Candace's meeting, which I felt pretty low about. And then I knew I had this appointment with the police (the police!) that afternoon—it kept me tense all day.

In my head I was picturing a police station as large as the Empire State Building. As it turned out, the local station was small and unimpressive looking, with what looked like dirty white bathroom tile on the walls. I showed up at quarter to three. Candace was already there.

"Where were you?" Candace asked, by way of greeting.

"Where was I when?"

As I've already explained, I can fool no one.

Candace just shook her head. "Wimp."

It was like auditions for a school play, we knew so many of the girls waiting on the long wooden benches, waiting to go in and see the cops. Candace knew *everyone*. She was signing up new members for her Find Jenny association right and left. She was working the crowd, getting everyone as angry about Jenny's disappearance as she was.

The first meeting, she informed me, had gone very well despite my absence. Jocelyn, our neighbor, worked at a copy shop and was going to run off hundreds of Find Jenny flyers for free.

Finally Candace came back to where I was standing.

"What's the matter?" she asked me. "You look like you just got arrested."

45

"This scares me."

"What does?"

"Being here."

"Ellie, did you ever notice that everything scares you?"

"That's a scary thought," I said.

"You should love this," Candace said. "You can soak up all kinds of details for your screenplay."

"I'm not writing any screenplay."

"Yes, you are. Don't say that. Don't be a jerk. I mean it, Ellie. You've got talent. Don't throw it in the garbage can. Hey. Promise me you'll finish a first draft by next week."

"Next week? Are you crazy? I can't write a screenplay in a week."

"Try."

When Candace said she was going to do something, she did it. Once, the previous year, she broke up with this track jock after he claimed that women's bodies just weren't built for sports. He insisted that Candace would never be able to run a six-minute mile, no matter how hard she tried. She told the jock she would run a six-minute mile by the end of the week. She trained like crazy for six straight days, and then with me sitting in the bleachers by the track in Riverside Park, timing her on a stopwatch, she broke the six-minute mark by two seconds. She didn't even bother to tell her ex-boyfriend she had done it, either. She said it was between herself and herself, a matter of keeping her own promise.

That was Candace. When I said I was going to do something, it was almost a way of guaranteeing to myself that I wouldn't do it. So Candace was always trying to be my coach, getting me to stick to my word.

46

"C'mon," she said. "Let's go snooping around. See if we can pick up anything."

"Why would you want to do a thing like that?"

"Ellie, Jenny could be out there somewhere, her life hanging by a thread. Don't you care about that?" She raised her voice enough to turn the heads of several girls sitting nearby. She looked mad.

I was going to remind her that she had already predicted Jenny was dead, but I thought she might start screaming at me.

Instead, she turned and headed off into the main floor of the station house, where all these police officers and detectives had their cluttered desks. First Candace went to the gray metal water fountain for a drink, and then she started wandering around among the desks. She started throwing little smiles back my way (at least she wasn't mad at me anymore). She kept tilting her head to indicate that I should join her. I made faces back to say "Be careful" or "What are you doing?" But she ignored me.

"Ellie."

I looked up and saw the familiar sad figure of Abby Rovere. She had always been plump, but she had gained weight over the summer. "Hey, Abby! So they called you, too, huh?"

"I just had my interview."

"How did it go?"

"It was so scary."

"Why?"

"Because they kept smiling at me and acting friendly, but all the time I could tell they were studying me and trying to figure me out and see inside me, you know what I mean?"

47

"I guess that's their job."

"Yeah, well, it scared me so much I wanted to confess."

"To what?"

"Anything. I wanted to say, 'Okay, okay, I did it. I killed Jenny.' What are *you* smiling about?"

"You really are crazier than me."

Candace was now hanging out by the fax machine. A cop came over and asked her what she was doing (she was too far away for me to hear what he asked her exactly, but that's what it looked like he asked her). I couldn't watch. I looked back at Abby. "So what was so bad about your summer?"

"Well, my parents got divorced. That's for starters."

"Oh, wow, I'm sorry."

"No, it's good. They were only staying together out of spite. And then, let's see, my dog died."

"You're kidding? Blackie?"

"Blackie is no more."

"I'm sorry."

"You don't look sorry."

"I know, I'm awful, but I can't help it. You just have the worst luck in the world."

"That *is* funny."

"How did Blackie die?"

"He was hit by a Domino's pizza delivery truck."

I burst out laughing.

"You really are the worst friend in the world, you know that?" Abby said. "Okay, let's see, what happened next?"

I peeked at Candace. She was smiling at the cop. They looked like they were now deep into some friendly discussion.

Abby said, "Then I called Seth about a hundred times."

Seth was this chubby homely business major whom Abby had pursued all second semester and who kept breaking up with her.

"He finally had his number changed," she said.

"Oh, no."

"I was so bummed I decided I wouldn't come back to school. Then I decided dropping out would be even more depressing than coming back, but by then it was too late to get a decent dorm assignment. So guess where I am this year? Plimpton."

"No."

"Yes."

Plimpton was the most dangerous Barnard dorm by far. It wasn't inside the fortress of the main campus, it was several blocks uptown. Girls going back to Plimpton after dark were strongly urged to take the security van.

"If you take the van, you'll be okay," I said. She looked doubtful. I added, "Just always, you know, take the van."

"I'm not going to be okay," Abby said. "I'm going to be next."

"Next? What are you talking about 'next'?"

"Next. Like Jenny. Like Lauren. Like Melita Sanchez. Next."

"That's a great attitude, Abby."

"Thank you. I'm kind of proud of it myself."

"Ellie Sommers and Candace Burkett?"

The man who had called my name was a thin guy in a greasy gray suit who had come out of some inner office.

"That's not the detective, is it?" I asked Abby.

"That's the detective," she said.

He wasn't what I was picturing as a detective at all. He was short, balding, more like an accountant than someone I'd want to hire to protect me.

I stood. "You want to wait for me?" I asked Abby.

"No, I gotta go try to find my sophomore adviser so she can tell me that I can't take any of the courses I want to take."

"Okay, I'll catch you later. Come by the apartment tonight."

Abby promised that she would and I headed down the hallway. Candace joined me on the way.

"Wait till you hear," she murmured in my ear.

"I'm Detective Pearl," the detective said, shaking first Candace's hand, then mine, and smiling. "Thanks for helping us out today."

"No problem," Candace said. She was giving me these mega-meaningful glances, which I found very unnerving, since the detective was standing right there.

The detective's office was nothing much. No window. There were some wanted posters taped up, with police sketches of scary criminal faces wearing ski caps. Why did all criminals seem to wear those things? Did they wear their ski caps when they committed crimes in the summer?

Standing in the corner, his hands in his pockets, was a large handsome older man with iron-gray hair, closely cropped. His suit was dark blue and in much better shape than Detective Pearl's. He looked about sixty. He also looked like Paul Newman. I stared at him, wide-eyed. This was more like what I had in mind when I imagined someone in the law-enforcement business. The man looked so serious and capable, so wise and fearless. Why can't you be my father? was the question that formed immediately in my mind.

My own dad was mostly bald, his tufts of gray hair

standing out on either side of his head like Bozo the clown. No—if I could cast someone in the role of daddy, I would have given it to this other man on the spot.

"Have a seat," Detective Pearl told us, waving his hand at the ratty-looking metal chairs in front of his desk. He sat behind his desk, coughed, and started fussing with papers. "Where did I—?"

"Here," said the older man, pointing to a Styrofoam cup of coffee hidden in the mess on Detective Pearl's desk.

"Ah, thank you." The detective took a long swig of coffee. "Garbage," he said, licking his lips. He smiled at us. "This," he said, hoisting the cup in the direction of the other man, "is FBI Special Agent Russell Wilkins. He's taking over as head of operations for the missing-persons cases at your school, helping us out a little while we look for Jenny Silver."

For the first time since I'd heard that Jenny was missing, I felt some hope that she would be found. The way this FBI man was standing, the way he was dressed—he had an aura about him, like he knew what he was doing and he got things done.

"Do you have any leads?" Candace asked. There wasn't a lot of respect in her voice. Instead, there was an edge, like she was about to sue them both for mishandling the case.

"Frankly, no," Detective Pearl said. If he had noticed the tone of Candace's question, he didn't seem to mind. "Now, what can you tell us about Jenny?"

"Anything at all would be helpful to us," said Agent Wilkins. It was the first thing he had said, and

I snapped my head sharply, staring. He had a deep gravelly voice. A perfect fatherly voice. I melted further.

Candace was telling them everything she could about Jenny Silver. Which was also everything that I could think of, as it turned out, so when it came to me I had very little to add. None of what Candace said sounded to me like it might be helpful, but Detective Pearl kept making notes.

"Who else did she talk to?" he asked.

"Talk to?" Candace asked.

"Hang out with, socialize with, talk to on the street . . ."

"How about someone older?" asked Agent Wilkins. "An older woman, say."

"Why?" Candace asked at once. "You think the killer is an old woman?"

"Whoa!" said Detective Pearl, holding up two hands. "Please. No one said anything about a killer."

"Well, you're a homicide detective, aren't you?" Candace said. "And the FBI doesn't exactly mess around with nickel-and-dime stuff, do they? Right, Ellie? Ellie's something of an expert on criminology."

"Oh, no, not really, I—"

"I mean, we're not babies, okay? Level with us. We know Jenny's probably dead."

"I pray to God that you're wrong," said Detective Pearl.

"Believe me," Agent Wilkins said, "we are doing everything we possibly can to find her."

"Yeah, well, that's what you always say, but I just don't understand what you guys have been doing, exactly," Candace said angrily. "You're telling me that

52

for five days you've been looking and you haven't come up with a single clue? I mean, how can a girl just vanish like that?"

"Candace," I said softly, "they're trying."

"How do you know?" she shot back. "How do we know they're giving this case any kind of priority?"

"Believe me, we are," Detective Pearl said.

"What are your credentials?" Candace asked him. "If you don't mind my asking."

Sometimes Candace went so far with her brash New Yorker style that I thought she'd get us into a fistfight, or worse. Now was one of those times. I grew up in a house where saying "Yes, please" was next to Godliness. I expected Detective Pearl to book us both for rudeness.

"I've been a detective for seven years," Detective Pearl said easily, "couple of medals, couple of citations. But Agent Wilkins here . . . we're very lucky he's come on this case, let me tell you. Girls, this is the man who caught the Mad Bomber of San Diego. And before that he bagged the Vampire Killer of Hollywood Hills."

I had heard about those killers, read the newspaper articles with a sick fascinated dread. And here was the man who had stopped them.

"He's something of a legend," Detective Pearl said with what sounded like genuine admiration. "Isn't that right, Agent Wilkins?"

"I had a lot of help on both those cases."

"So as far as credentials go—"

"If you think the killer is an old lady," Candace went on, unfazed, "then you should get the word out so everyone can be more careful. Jesus! Don't you even care that a girl is missing? Don't you

53

care that one of us—me! or Ellie here!—we could be next?"

Detective Pearl had a slight smile on his face. "Ms. Burkett," he said, "I know you're upset and angry because you're worried about your friend. This may be hard for you to believe, but I feel the same way. This isn't just a job to me. I want to do everything in my power to find that girl. And so does the FBI. Now, I don't know why you've gotten all hooked on this old-lady idea, but let me tell you something. On a case like this, we've always got theories working. Okay? They change day by day. We don't release that information to the press because A) it could scare a lot of people for no reason, and B) which is much more important, if we happen to be right about something, some little detail, we may not want to tip our hand to some crazy psycho out there because we need a certain element of surprise on our side. You understand?"

His nice manner had disappeared. There was a hard cold glint in the detective's eyes. He was staring right at Candace, but I felt scared anyway. I remembered what Abby had said. She was right. The way he was looking at Candace—and through her at the same time—I suddenly wanted to confess to killing Jenny.

"Did I make my point here?" Detective Pearl asked.

"Sure," Candace said, unflinchingly meeting his gaze.

The FBI agent took out his wallet and handed us each a small crisp card with his name and number. "If you think of anything more, anything at all, please feel free to call. Anytime."

"Thank you," I said, giving him a big grin. "Oh," I

said, "we forgot to tell them about the Find Jenny group."

Candace glared at me as I belatedly realized that she had left this out on purpose. It was too late now. I told the two men about the group that Candace was organizing.

The detective glanced at Agent Wilkins; they exchanged frowns. "Putting up flyers is one thing," Detective Pearl said. "But please, I beg you, don't try anything else."

"The main thing we want you girls to concentrate on right now is taking every security precaution you can," Agent Wilkins agreed. "We certainly don't want you knocking on doors and exposing yourself to unnecessary danger."

"Is there a serial killer out there?" Candace asked, looking Detective Pearl right in the eye.

The detective looked at the FBI agent again.

"Honestly, we don't know," Agent Wilkins said. "We hope that there isn't, obviously, but we have to act as if there is, just in case."

Agent Wilkins spread his large hands wide, as if waiting to catch a basketball. "Here's the thing, Candace. If there is someone out there stalking the campus, then they're going to strike again when they get the chance. Do me a favor. Don't give them a chance, okay?"

That was good enough for me. I was taking the 3:58 bus back to Englewood.

CHAPTER 7

"WHAT'S THE MATTER WITH YOU?" I ASKED
Candace when we were out on the street again.

"What's the matter with me? What were you making goo-goo eyes at them for?"

That stung. "I was just being polite."

"Any authority figure and you're a puddle,"
Candace said.

"That's not . . . untrue," I admitted. Because she
was so right. I was a total sucker for mentor figures.
Can you blame me? A pair of horribly unhappy parents don't make for the greatest role models; they
kind of leave you hungering for more.

"But what were you giving me all those looks for?"
I asked.

"I'll tell you in a sec."

She was walking even faster than usual, and I had
to work hard to keep up. She didn't tell me what was
going on until we had sat down in a booth in Tom's
Diner, which was extremely cheap and our personal
favorite local restaurant.

"Okay," she said. She looked around again, making sure no one was watching. "I read this fax while we were in there."

"What kind of fax?

"A fax, you know, about the case. About Jenny."

"You read a private police fax?"

"A little louder, wouldya? I don't think everyone in the diner heard you."

"Candace, are you psycho or what?"

"Now, let's see if I can remember everything. It was from something called the BSU."

"The BSU? In Virginia?"

"Yeah, Quantico."

"Candace, that's the Psyche Squad."

"The what?"

"I read about them this summer. That's a branch of the FBI. The Behavioral Sciences Unit."

"You see?" Candace said with a grin. "That screenplay of yours is coming in handy already."

A young Latino busboy plopped two glasses of ice water on the table between us. Candace guzzled hers. I stared at her hand. She was wearing a beautiful new ring, a silver mermaid whose long silver hair twined around until it joined the mermaid's tail.

"Where'd you get this ring?" I asked, pulling her hand toward me so I could study the mermaid up close.

"The Village." She pulled her hand free. "What's the Behavioral Sciences Unit?"

"Do you think they'd have another one?"

"Ellie!"

"They're these FBI agents who study criminal behavior and the criminal mind. They don't even visit the crime scenes a lot of the time. They just

57

study the files and try to get into the mind of the killer and make guesses about what the killer might be like. They say it's really hard work, too, because the agents have to spend the whole day thinking and feeling like killers. It's sort of like what writers go through, you know, trying to become all their different characters."

"No wonder the FBI has no leads on the case," said Candace. "Jesus. What a lot of bull."

"No, listen," I said, "the BSU actually has this amazing track record. One time they were able to tell the cops that this certain serial killer drove a rusty car and lived with his parents. They pinpointed his location within a two-mile radius and those were enough clues for the cops to find the killer the very next day."

Candace's green eyes were gleaming. "So then what I saw is even more important than I thought. It was a new profile—"

My mouth dropped open.

"—of a possible serial killer in the missing-persons cases of Leiter, Sanchez, and Silver."

"Oh my God! Oh my God!"

"I told you it was worth snooping around."

"You read this? What did it say?"

"I didn't get to read the whole thing, but first of all it said a lot of stuff about how speculative this whole profile is because they don't have any dead bodies in this case. Yet."

That last word chilled me thoroughly.

"Then it said something about the killer being highly organized, I remember that. It sounded pretty weird to me. What do they mean? They think the killer's room is neat?"

"Sort of." I explained. Organized versus disorganized—it was one of the BSU's main distinctions about killers. A disorganized killer was so demented he didn't even plan his crimes or take any precautions for covering them up. A disorganized killer might not even hide his dead bodies. Or you might see him on the day of a killing walking around with bloodstained clothes.

"Nice," said Candace.

"Well, in a way, it *is* nice, because it's easier to catch someone like that."

An organized killer was more methodical, hiding everything.

Candace thought about this. "So how come they're saying this killer is organized?"

I thought, too. "Well, that makes sense, because they haven't found the bodies, like you said."

"Yeah yeah yeah," Candace said, snapping her fingers. "There was something in the fax about that. They figure the killer must have a way of thoroughly disposing of the victims' bodies. But get this, it also said they think the killer is probably keeping souvenirs."

The first thing that flashed in my head were those little plastic key chains with a map of New Jersey that they sold at all the rest stops on the interstate. Then I pictured the souvenirs the FBI had in mind and felt my teeth grinding.

"Now why would they say that?" Candace asked.

"Because they know from experience that serial killers do that. These wackos like to relive their moments of triumph," I said. "So they keep something, like one of Jenny's ears say."

"Make me puke."

59

"I know. And then on those lonely nights when they wish they could be out slitting some girl's throat but they don't have the courage? They sit around kissing the dead ear and remembering how powerful they are, picturing the terror in the eyes of their victim, that kind of thing."

I couldn't go on. I had now scared myself so completely that I was having to concentrate on not wetting my pants.

"That is truly gross," Candace said. "Souvenirs. My God."

Candace and I stared at each other.

"What?" I said.

She didn't answer.

"Is there more?" I asked.

She nodded.

"Don't tell me."

"You already know it. They tipped us in the interview."

My mind remained utterly blank.

Then Candace said, "They're thinking it could be a woman."

I don't know why, but this news really threw me. A woman. It was as if the killer was no longer Out There but suddenly was someone inside my own camp.

"They didn't have my name down, did they?" I joked.

"No, they're not thinking it's someone like us. Someone older, someone . . ."

"What? What what what?"

"Someone we know very well, someone we all look up to, and trust."

"You're kidding me."

Because if someone had specifically designed a

torture for me, Miss Always-Looking-for-a-Mentor, they couldn't have done better than the BSU's killer profile.

"That's why Agent Wilkins asked me that about Jenny talking to older women. They think the killer may be some whacked-out old lady," Candace said.

And as she said it I suddenly realized we were no longer alone.

We both looked up.

The old woman's haggard face was staring right down at us with beady bloodstained eyes.

CHAPTER 8

I GASPED.

"What'll you have?" Arlene asked in a low, bored voice.

Arlene was this seventy-year-old waitress and a Tom's regular whom we knew well from last year. We had fought with her so often (over eggs that had gone cold or waffles that were soggy) that we had grown fond of her in a perverse way.

"Don't we even get a hello?" Candace asked. "Or a welcome back?"

"Hello, welcome back, what'll you have?"

Candace ordered a burger deluxe. I didn't feel like eating all of a sudden. Arlene frowned at me.

"There's a five-dollar minimum on the tables."

"I'm getting ten dollars' worth, don't worry," Candace told her.

"Per person," Arlene said.

"All right," I said. "Tuna on rye and a chocolate shake."

I figured I could always have it wrapped to go.

"It's her," I said after the waitress left. "Arlene.

She's killing Barnard students who don't leave big tips."

"Very funny," Candace said with a frown. She reached in her pocket and scattered a handful of change on the tabletop. She picked out a quarter. "I'm going to go call *The New York Times*."

"Why?" I asked, though I knew why.

"I'm going to get this news out there. About the profile, tell them who the cops suspect."

"Didn't you hear what the detective said? You could mess up their entire investigation."

"I don't care about that. I care about protecting Barnard students."

Sometimes Candace sounded like she was running for political office, which she was probably going to do for real someday.

"Candace, listen to me, if you mess up their investigation and let the killer get away, that's not going to help anybody."

Candace was standing, quarter in hand. "I'm calling," she said.

"Okay, but you could end up being responsible for people dying," I said.

She spun the quarter on the table. "Heads I call," she said.

The coin came up tails.

"Don't call," I said, because I saw the look on her face and I knew she was still thinking about it.

"Okay, okay, okay, so maybe I won't. But that fax is going to help us in our investigation, that's the important thing."

"Our investigation?"

"Ellie, I'm sorry, but I'm not going to let you be a total wuss-head on this one. This is Jenny, a girl we

63

know. We have to do everything we can to help."

"I'm going home."

"Why? You're not hungry?"

"No, not home to the apartment, home home, Englewood. I mean, didn't you hear him? There may be a serial killer on the loose."

Candace spun the quarter again. This time it came up heads. It came up heads two more times before she spoke again.

"Ellie, if you run away from this I will never speak to you again. And that's not just a threat, it's a fact."

I could tell Candace meant it, and it pained me greatly. In fact, I wanted to cry.

I was at a crossroads. In books, people have a revelation and then they're changed forever. With me, it felt like I kept having the same revelation and facing the same crossroads over and over again, and it never got easier to cross to the other side. I stared at my hands. "Okay," I mumbled finally, "I'll stay."

Candace smiled at me so proudly I almost felt brave. "What are you doing tonight?" she asked.

"Uh, nothing, why?"

"I've got a plan, how maybe we can catch this crazy old broad."

CHAPTER 9

THAT NIGHT I STAYED BUSY SETTING UP MY room and praying that Candace would forget about whatever it was she had in mind.

Candace had said she'd take the smaller bedroom, which she said had better light and was closer to the bathroom. So I had the large master bedroom in back with the gated window that opened onto the fire escape. Through the gate, and through a gap between two large buildings, I could see the AR part of a neon bar sign on Amsterdam Avenue, flashing on and off.

I unpacked my little TV, plugged it in, and on came yet another report about Jenny's disappearance on Channel 4. "Tonight the parents of missing Barnard teenager Jennifer Silver offer a large reward for information. . . ."

And then there were Mr. and Mrs. Silver tearfully offering a $50,000 reward to anyone with information about their daughter's whereabouts. The whole time they were talking and crying, a number was projected across the bottom of the screen: 1-800-22JENNY.

The news program also reported that Barnard had beefed up campus security beyond its already high level. Nevertheless, seven Barnard girls had already dropped out of school.

Even before the report ended, my mom called, of course. I was on the phone with her for an hour, trying to convince her that I was safe and that it was okay for me to stay in New York.

Barnard is a small school, only about five hundred girls in each year's class. But that's still a big enough student body to make seven dropouts sound puny. Privately I prayed that everyone would drop out. Then the administration would have to close the place down and I could go home without looking cowardly.

"So you're staying?" my mother asked in a trembly voice.

What could I say? Not only was I staying, but Candace had elected me co-deputy of her search party.

When my little digital alarm clock flipped past eleven-thirty, I was sure I was in the clear and that Candace had forgotten about her plan. But at 11:32 she wandered into my room with her head down as she ripped apart a little shrink-wrapped package.

"What's that?" I asked warily. I felt like I do at the doctor's office when the nurse comes in carrying a big syringe.

She handed me a funny-looking pen. "Pepper spray. You spray it in the mugger's eyes and it immobilizes them. I would have gotten Mace but it's illegal in New York State."

I sat up, took the pen. I held it away from my body as if it might bite me.

"I can't believe they would make Mace illegal,"

Candace said with disgust. "Everyone bends over back-ward to protect the criminals. No one cares about the victims." She sat on the bed next to me, grabbed my bare foot, and squeezed it. "Which is what you and I are not going to become. You hear me?"

I smiled weakly. "Pepper spray, huh? With my luck the killer will just start sneezing."

Candace gave me a look. "You should probably take it out onto the quad tomorrow and practice with it, but take it with you tonight just to be safe. I've got one, too."

Here we go, I thought.

"Tonight?"

Candace got up and wandered out into the living room. Her voice floated back to me. "My plan, remember?"

Though I didn't want to, I followed her. "Which is?"

"I'll tell you in a minute." She crossed to the kitchen and rummaged around till she found this battered manila file folder (it was hidden under a box of pots and pans we still hadn't unpacked). She started reading.

I was immediately terrified. What was she reading? I was afraid to ask.

"You know, I don't really understand their think-ing on this one," I said, flopping down on the sofa. "The BSU, I mean. You sure they're thinking old woman? Most serial killers are young white men."

Partly I was truly interested in brainstorming about the case, but partly (a bigger part) I was attempting my old tried-and-true high-school trick for getting out of unpleasant homework assignments—keep the teacher talking.

Candace looked up from her reading. "Oh, yeah, it said something about that in the fax."

"Now she tells me."

"You just reminded me. They figure from the way this killer is spacing out the kills—you know, so far apart—that she's calm and unflappable, doesn't need a lot of publicity, stuff like that. It said that might—*might*—point to someone older."

"Okay," I said, mulling this over. "I could maybe buy that." I certainly liked the idea that the killer wouldn't be killing again for a while. "Also," I said, "in a way, it makes sense that the killer would be an old woman, because who would be afraid of someone like that?"

"What do you mean?"

"Well, the way these girls disappeared, you got to figure somebody won their trust, even just for a minute. We're all programmed to watch out for dangerous men, right? But an old woman? That's Grandma. That's safe."

Especially at a women's college like Barnard, where we all looked up to the older women on the faculty like gods. Goddesses, I should say.

"Okay," I said. "I agree with them now."

"Mmm," Candace said. She wasn't listening.

"But how could an old lady be powerful enough to do anything to us?" I wondered.

"Maybe it's a big old lady."

I had a terrifying thought. "Like old Molly?" I asked.

"Yeah, like old Molly," Candace agreed, her head still buried in what she was reading.

"Like old Molly?" I said again.

Candace stared at me. "You mean, as in, old Molly

is the killer? Good going, Detective. That makes a lot of sense."

"Why not? She's kind of nutty."

"Yeah, but Molly is great."

Molly had already been up to our apartment twice, once to unstick a window that was painted shut and once just to see how we were doing. She had bustled around the place, filled with good cheer; it had felt good having her around. But . . .

"Are you sure?" I asked.

"Ellie, if there were dead Columbia guys showing up, especially guys who had tried to sneak into the building late at night, then you'd have something. But why would Molly hurt Barnard girls? She wants to protect us. It's the wrong motive. I thought you were supposed to be a writer."

"I'm not a writer, I can't write a thing."

"Well, you're convincing me, because motive is one of the most important things you gotta establish in a mystery; even I know that."

"What are you reading over there?"

"Fran Calder gave me her notes on Jenny."

Fran was a student reporter for the *Spectator*. She was the one who had written the editorial last spring that had inspired my failed screenplay. She had joined Candace's Find Jenny club.

Candace snapped the file shut. She looked at her watch. "Okay," she said. "Let's go."

My heart sank.

"We're going to follow Jenny's route," Candace explained. "As best we can."

"Now? It's almost midnight."

"Exactly. I want to do it at the same time she did."

"Oh, great thinking."

"It is good thinking. If the killer has certain habits or patterns, we want to fit right in."

"Candace, may I remind you that the killer has a certain pattern we don't want to fit right into? Namely killing?"

"It's the only way I can think of to find her."

I'm ashamed to admit this, but I actually felt like throwing up.

"Ellie," Candace said patiently, "we're going to be together. That's not going to be a very tempting target, especially if the FBI is right about their killer profile. An old lady couldn't take us both at once."

"Very comforting."

She looked at her watch again. "Let's go," she said.

New York is known as the city that never sleeps. It's not true. Outside it was raining slightly, misting really. And as we walked back to the Barnard campus, the streets were deserted. No homeless people selling rained-on paperbacks and used clothes on the sidewalks. No crowds out strolling, enjoying the smoggy humid air. Just an occasional pedestrian looming up at us suddenly from out of the shadows and then hurrying on.

If they had wanted to, anyone we passed could have mugged us no problem, pepper spray or no pepper spray.

Jenny and Karen Braverhoff had been rooming together in Hewitt, part of the triumvirate of dorms known as BHR. That was on the main campus, so we started from Barnard's front gates. We walked one block, then crossed the street to the all-night deli. The Korean owner was sitting outside on a plastic milk crate, slicing oranges for the little fruit cups he sold

70

for a buck apiece. We went inside. There was a young Korean woman behind the register. She said hello.

When Candace bought a pint of Ben & Jerry's, I got a very creepy feeling. She had bought Cherry Garcia. We were following in Jenny's footsteps, just like Candace had said we would. And those footsteps led to oblivion.

Outside the grocery, we stood watching the occasional taxi whiz by in the rain. Around us the tall massive buildings rose like a dark canyon. Candace was frowning. "Now what?" she wondered.

"We go home and eat the ice cream," I suggested.

She didn't laugh. "C'mon," she said, "we gotta stay serious. What have we learned so far?"

"That the killer must have met Jenny inside the store," I said.

"We don't know that for sure."

"I think we do."

"Okay, so let's say that's true. What does it tell us?"

"Well, if it is an old lady, maybe she asked Jenny to help her across the street, or help her home with her groceries," I suggested.

"Nah. Then the shopkeepers would have seen them together and told that to the cops. But all they told the cops was that Jenny left the store, remember?"

"Which means," I said, "the killer must have stopped her on the way back to campus."

We looked across the street. Not much room for a killer to maneuver in.

And right then I thought of something. "Just a sec," I said. I went back inside the store. Candace followed me. I went over to the fridge section where they kept the sodas and other drinks. There were plastic strips hanging down to keep in the cold air. I pulled back the strips, staring at the shelves.

"What?" Candace said from over my shoulder.

I ignored her. "Do you have Yoo-Hoo?" I asked the woman behind the register.

"No Yoo-Hoo," she said.

When I turned around, Candace was giving me such an excited look it made my heart pound. "You're a genius," she told me.

"You don't carry it?" Candace asked the shop-keeper.

"No carry," she said with a shrug. "Sorry."

We hurried out of the store. "Genius, genius, genius," Candace said.

I felt so proud it almost made up for how scared I was. "You see," I said, "those stupid questions I always ask aren't so stupid after—"

"You're right," Candace interrupted, not wanting to waste any more time on compliments. "So Jenny couldn't find Karen's Yoo-Hoo. So what store would she try next?"

We looked down Broadway. "I guess we should just start walking down Broadway and see what's open," I said.

We walked slowly. I had come up with something that maybe the cops hadn't thought of—and that only scared me more. I felt sure we were now going to walk straight into the arms of the killer.

We tried two more stores. No Yoo-Hoo.

"Would she keep going or would she turn back?" Candace asked.

"She'd keep going," I said. "Jenny was as sweet as a Girl Scout."

"Right."

We were at the corner of 111th. I was about to walk on, but Candace was staring down the cross street. She reached out and held my arm, which made me want to scream.

"Look," she said.

Just around the corner there was one of those seedy buildings owned by the city and used to house the homeless, many of whom were outpatients dumped from the state's mental institutions. There were several crazy-looking people hanging around out front, sitting on the stoop. Next to the stoop one of the tenants was sitting in a dilapidated wheelchair. . . .

An old woman.

CHAPTER 10

"OKAY," I WHISPERED. "I'VE SEEN ENOUGH, let's call the cops."

"And say what? We spotted a woman in a wheelchair?"

"That's good enough for me."

But Candace was already walking down the street. I followed. What else could I do?

"Hi," Candace told the old woman.

The woman looked up, eyeing Candace coldly, not saying a word. The other people sitting on the steps of the building glanced our way, then went back to their noisy arguments and discussions. One heavyset man was drinking something out of a paper bag. I smelled liquor. Then I smelled rotting garbage. I spotted the open cans by the street. Just my luck, I was in time to see a large hairy rat scurry away from the cans and go running toward the sewer.

"How are you tonight?" Candace asked the old woman.

"Horrible." Her voice was a raspy squawk.

"I'm sorry to hear that. What's wrong?"

"Don't ask. Want some advice? Don't ever grow old, that's my advice to you." She chuckled bitterly. Her bony hands were fidgeting with each other in her lap. "Look what happens. You see all your friends die. You get abandoned by your children. You end up in a dump like this."

"Listen," Candace said, "we were wondering if by any chance you might have seen a friend of ours? She's about this tall and she's thin and—"

She launched into a description of Jenny Silver. The old woman didn't appear to be listening. She had turned her bony head to stare at me. With her wrinkled dewlapped neck and her partially bald head she reminded me of a vulture.

"Never seen her," she croaked when Candace finished.

"You sure?"

"What? You think I would lie to you?" The old woman grinned toothlessly. "How old would you say I am?"

"Uh"—Candace pretended to size her up—"fifty?"

"I'm seventy-six."

"Wow," Candace said, "I never would have guessed you were that old. Would you, Ellie?"

The woman looked closer to ninety. "No way," I agreed, wishing that Candace hadn't used my real name. Two people had already left the steps, heading back inside the building. Now the heavyset guy with the bag of liquor finished his bottle. He tossed the bottle into the open trash cans where it landed with a crash. "What a shot," he mumbled to himself. Then he stumbled down the steps and weaved off down the street.

Which left me and Candace alone with the old-woman serial psycho killer.

I started shifting back and forth from foot to foot.

"You have to go to the bathroom or something?" the old woman asked me.

"No, no," I said, blushing.

"She's a nervous type," Candace said.

"Sure she's nervous," said the old woman. "City like this . . . it's a jungle, believe me. And pretty young girls like you . . . everyone wants you when you're a young pretty girl. Sure. Everyone wants a piece of you. Everyone wants to grab at you."

She made bird beaks with her hands and pinched the air.

"That's why you've got to be very very careful, believe me," she said. "Listen to me. Be very very careful. Oh dear God, you know what I wouldn't give to be young again like you? I'd kill to be young like you."

Motive.

"What's your name?" Candace asked bluntly.

The old woman looked flattered. "Esther. Esther Green."

"Nice to meet you, Esther. I'm Candace. And this is Ellie Sommers."

Great. Now she had my whole name. . . .

"So this is where you live, huh?" Candace asked, glancing up at the building.

"This is the place. This is my palace. It's filled with crackheads and junkies and prostitutes and every other vile kind of lowlife. This is home."

"Candace," I said, "I really think we better be—"

"Listen," the old woman interrupted. "Can I ask you a favor?"

We both turned to look at her. There was a shrewd look in the woman's beady eyes that disturbed me greatly.

"What?" Candace asked.

"My daughter wheeled me out here so I could soak up some of this nice polluted air. She was supposed to wheel me back in an hour ago, but she went off somewhere. I've got arthritis in these arms, you wouldn't believe it. I can't even bend them some days. I can't get out of the chair unless somebody carries me. I'm going to get mugged if I keep sitting out here, but there's no way I can push myself up that ramp. Would you do me a favor and push me back into my apartment?"

My heart stopped beating.

"It'll only take a minute."

Right then I knew for sure. This was Jenny's killer.

I knew how Jenny had died, too, or at least part of the story. Jenny had helped the old woman inside.

"Please," the old woman said.

I was about to run, but Candace said, "Sure, of course, we'll help you. Right, Ellie?"

CHAPTER 11

"CANDACE," I SAID, "WE DON'T HAVE TIME!"

"Why not?"

"Because we have to get back for that . . . phone call."

"What phone call?"

I couldn't think of a way out of the corner I had painted myself into. I'm terrible in situations like this. I become freeze-dried in the brain. "*The* phone call," I said helplessly.

"It'll just take a second, right?" Candace asked Esther.

"Just a second of your time," she agreed. "You've got lots of time, now, don't you? Young pretty girls like yourselves."

Candace had turned the wheelchair around and was pushing Esther up the creaky wooden ramp next to the steps. That meant that Esther had her back to us, and I took the opportunity to nudge Candace and make my face go absolutely berserk. Candace ignored me. I looked down; Esther had turned her head to look up at me over her shoulder, so she caught the faces I was making.

"Sure," she said, turning frontward again, "you don't want to bother with an old lady like me, I know. I smell bad, I'm ugly, I got nothing to talk about. Why would you want to hang out with me?"

"No, no," I said helplessly, "it's just we're . . . in a rush."

The entrance foyer was covered with graffiti. The mailboxes had been pried open like sardine cans.

"I'm on the first floor, right here," said Esther. "Thank God for small favors, am I right?" She laughed hysterically, as if this were the greatest joke ever told.

I heard someone shouting at the end of the hall. It sounded like there was a fistfight going on. Someone was throwing furniture around. "See? A madhouse," Esther said. "This is where my lousy daughter lets me live."

She fumbled in her lap, her hands shaking. She produced—

A gun?

No, a key, which she held out to Candace. Candace opened the door and was about to push her inside. I grabbed her arm.

"There you go," I told the old woman. "You're in now."

"Come on," I whispered fiercely to Candace.

"Oh now, you've got to at least take a toffee," the old lady called, "and a cup of coffee. Toffee and coffee. I rhymed! And if you could wheel me in front of the TV, I'd really appreciate it. Otherwise I'll just be staring at the roaches on the walls until my daughter has the decency to come back here, which could be never, knowing her."

79

Candace said, "Sure," and bumped the wheelchair over the threshold.

The apartment was a studio with ugly stucco walls that felt like they were closing in on me. I saw the roaches Esther was talking about. The roaches were braver and more confident than I was; they didn't even scurry now that the lights were on. The TV was old and battered. Candace wheeled the old woman in front of it, turned it on. On came a blurry city news report—highlights from the day's new batch of horrible crimes.

"The candy is on the coffee table," the old woman said. "Take one."

The dish of candy was porcelain and fancy. The candy looked dusty and ancient. Candace took one, I didn't.

"Eat it," the old woman said.

I was horrified to see that Candace was unwrapping the candy and putting it in her mouth. "Mmm—delicious," she said.

"That's my daughter there," Esther said, waving a bony hand at the wall where a fuzzy photo hung at an angle. The woman in the picture looked like she was in her fifties and heavy. I glanced around the room in a sudden panic. What if the daughter . . .

The room was empty.

"Well," I said again.

But Candace had walked over to see the picture up close. "Oh, she's very beautiful," she said.

"She's not," Esther said. "Not in that picture anyway. Wait, I think I have a better one."

I heard movement.

I turned back slowly. I was too scared to move any quicker.

80

It was like in a dream, when you suddenly find yourself trying to flee through a sea of molasses.

And there she was—

The old woman.

She had gotten up out of her wheelchair.

She started walking toward us.

CHAPTER 12

"HEY," CANDACE SAID WITH AN EASY GRIN. "I thought you said you couldn't get out of the wheelchair by yourself."

The old woman grinned back. "That's my little secret. I lied about that. It's the only way I can get my daughter to visit me at all. Now, where was that picture? You know what? I bet it's in the back of that closet over there. If you two girls would just—"

"We have to go now," I said loudly and firmly.

Candace looked at me, and for once she listened.

"Yeah," she agreed. "We really do have to leave now, but it sure was nice meeting you."

Two spry steps and the old woman was by the door, blocking our way out. Okay, I told myself. She's little. I can knock her down if I have to. What could she have on her? A gun? In my pocket I closed my hand into a sweaty fist around my pepper pen.

"You're not going anywhere," the old woman said harshly.

Candace laughed. "Sorry," she said. "Maybe we'll come by another night."

She tried to shoulder past Esther to the door, but Esther wouldn't budge and Candace didn't want to hurt her.

Hurt her! I almost screamed.

The old woman's face had suddenly become red with fury. "You little brats! Sure! Run away! What do you care about an old lady like me? What do you care? Run! You filthy little brats! You'll get what's coming to you if I have anything to do with it. Abandoning an old lady. Don't you have a heart? Don't you have any decency? Wait till you get to be my age, you filthy little brats! You hear what I'm saying to you? *Do you?*"

I heard. By then Candace had gently but firmly moved Esther out of the doorway. We hurried out into the hall. And now we were moving fast for the front door as the old woman continued to scream at us.

I looked back once. The old lady was stamping her little foot. Her mouth was wide-open. I could see her tongue as she yelled. Her face was now bloodred.

We called Agent Wilkins as soon as we got home. He promised to check out Esther Green and call us back. In the meantime he made *us* promise not to go out of our apartment again that night.

Agent Wilkins called us back the next morning.

"Esther Green didn't have anything to do with Jenny's disappearance," he said.

"But that can't be," I said. "It's got to be her."

Last night I had been so sure that we had caught the killer. I believed that the terror was over.

On the other hand, if Esther Green wasn't the

83

killer, it might mean that Jenny was still alive. But I wasn't thinking that way. Selfishly, I felt only an intense disappointment—and fear.

"Are you sure?" I asked weakly.

"First of all," Agent Wilkins said, "until three days ago, Esther Green was in a mental hospital. She wasn't taking her medication and her daughter made her go. That's for starters."

Candace had come out of her bedroom in her underwear, an excited question mark written across her sleepy face. I shook my head.

"What about the other two?" I asked miserably.

"Leiter and Sanchez? That old lady has only been mainstreamed out of the institution for one year, so she's off the hook for both of those cases as well."

"Oh."

"Ellie?"

"Yes."

"Remember what Detective Pearl told you two about doing any investigating on your own?"

"Uh-huh."

"I can't emphasize that enough. You wandered into a crazy woman's apartment last night. She may not have had anything to do with Jenny Silver's disappearance, but she could have ended up having everything to do with your disappearance, you understand me?"

"Yes."

"The sad fact is, there are a lot of sickos in this city. Not just one. But," he said with a sigh, "all I can do is warn you. I can plead with you to be careful. That's all I can do. I can't make you take precautions. I can't make you protect yourself. You understand?"

"Yes, Daddy," I felt like saying.

Instead what I said was "Thank you, Sir. It won't happen again, I promise you."

And then I hung up.

Candace was sitting at the kitchen table. Neither of us said a word. She opened the Life cereal box, tipped it out over a bowl. A few yellow crumbs sprinkled out. The box was empty.

"You . . . stupid . . ."

I began quietly. I was shocked by what I was feeling. My anger seemed to come from nowhere; it was as if my emotion was a killer that had snuck up behind me and hit me with an ax. "You stupid fool!" I finished loudly.

Candace blinked. Her pretty oval face was still as marble. "I beg your pardon?"

"You heard me."

"Yeah, I did, but I don't really have any idea what you're mad about, so if you don't mind—"

"What am I mad about? What am I mad about! I'm mad about last night, you—you *moron*! I'm mad about your crazy plan!"

The night before I had been more scared than I'd ever been in my life. And I guess all that tension had stayed inside me through the night, even while I slept. And now that I found out that Esther Green was not the old lady we were looking for, and that we had risked our lives for nothing, the tension just burst out of me. I was shouting.

Pretty soon Candace started shouting back about what a baby I was.

"Don't you understand?" I shrieked. "You could have gotten us *killed. Killed.* Don't you get it?"

It was the worst fight we'd ever had. That wasn't saying much. We almost never fought.

85

I apologized an hour later when I had calmed down. But I made it clear that I wasn't doing anything like we had done last night ever again. Ever ever ever ever.

But, as I already told you . . .

I have trouble sticking to my word.

CHAPTER 13

THOSE FIRST FEW WEEKS OF SCHOOL WENT by in about five minutes. There was so much to do. Which was lucky, because it kept my mind off the serial killer who might be lurking in every dark alley waiting to strangle me to death. That kind of thing.

Mainly I spent my time going to the movies with Abby and fixing up the apartment. Once or twice I went to the cavernous Columbia gym (the Barnard gym consisted of a grotty basketball court and a pool the size of a large bathtub), where I swam a few lazy laps. Also, of course, I was going to classes and doing homework. We were still in that shopping period when you were allowed to switch classes and you were encouraged to try as many different professors as you could. I didn't do that, of course, cowardly creature of habit that I am. I just stuck with the first classes I tried, whether I liked them or not.

Even though my major was English, I was taking a Columbia course, Elements of Mathematical Logic, with Professor David Birnbaum, who was an old friend of my father's. My father had never given up the hope that I would decide to be a mathematician like himself. The truth was, I loved math, I just couldn't bear the thought of going into the same profession as Dad. On the other hand, I also couldn't bear the thought of disappointing him, so I kept taking one math class every semester.

I had convinced Abby to take the logic class with me so we'd have at least one class together, and we'd already spent hours drawing big circular Venn diagrams and puzzling over complex problems in set theory.

Those first weeks I also hung out with Candace, when she was around. We were getting along again. But after our screaming argument the morning that Agent Wilkins called, we didn't talk about Jenny Silver much. In fact, we declared a moratorium on the whole topic.

Between us, that is. With her other friends, Candace never talked about anything else. Seemed like her Find Jenny club met almost every night, too. They made up more flyers and went around pasting and stapling them to bulletin boards and bus kiosks all over the city. And so Jenny's picture was added to the ghoulish gallery that included Lauren Leiter and Melita Sanchez. In my own superstitious gloomy way, I concluded they were sealing Jenny's doom by adding her picture to the others that way. But of course I didn't say so. It was bad enough that I didn't come to the meetings.

At least, Candace didn't question me about that. After our night of terror, I felt half-justified. Like I had already done enough.

The apartment was really shaping up. Once we set up our bookcases in the entrance hallway, you almost had to walk sideways to get in. But other than that, the place was pretty cozy.

After what had happened to Jenny, I thought I wouldn't be able to sleep, I'd be so afraid of psychos sneaking up the fire escape, crowbarring the gate and killing me. But strangely enough, from that first night on I slept like a baby.

In a way I think it was a relief to be back in Manhattan. New York at night is a unique and noisy experience. There's this incessant traffic noise. And then there are these occasional middle-of-the-night arguments out on the street. And every now and then you hear the sound of glass breaking; it happens too often to bother worrying about it, or at least it's too often to call the police every time.

In Englewood, we were all alone in a big empty house. Every creak the house made sent my blood pressure up another five points. At least in New York there'd be plenty of people around if anything happened. Plenty of neighbors to hear your screams and not do anything about it.

There was another factor buoying me up. I had survived my little night of detective work with Candace. To me, that felt like a major accomplishment and relief. I had concluded that the whole business was somehow over. I was in the clear.

Besides, Candace gave off confidence like a bright light. Basking in her glory, I felt confident myself. And safe.

And then one night I came home and found the door of the apartment ajar.

I froze, my hand in midair on its way to sticking the key in the lock.

Then I heard the voices and the laughter inside

the apartment and my blood began to move again; I pushed the door open and went in.

Candace was in the kitchen, arranging a big bouquet of long-stem roses in my crystal pitcher (one of the many things my mother had insisted I take from home this year to help furnish the place). The rose petals were so red they looked as if they were drenched with blood. Grady was leaning against the dining-room table, hands in his pockets, nervous grin on his face. He didn't look pleased to see me, even though he smiled and said, "Ellie Sommers, now there's a sight for sore eyes."

"Hey, Ellie," Candace said (she looked very pleased to see me), "look at the beautiful flowers Grady brought me."

"Wow, gorgeous."

"It's my little way of trying to get Candace to go out with me again," Grady said, smiling at Candace. When she looked away, he added with a forced chuckle, "Or at least go out with me tonight."

Usually Candace didn't break up with guys, she just gently suggested that she didn't feel *that* way about them. Her reasons always sounded minor to boyfriendless me. With Grady, Candace was turned off by his southern chivalry, always opening the door for her, that kind of thing. Then one night in the cafeteria he had entered into the table's debate on some feminist topic or other. He said he thought that the women's movement had done many women a disservice by making them feel that being a housewife somehow wasn't enough. That had sealed Grady's fate forever.

Candace put the roses on the table, moving too quickly for Grady to put his arms around her, then

90

headed back into the kitchen, where she made herself busy with the wine he had brought.

"Hey," I said, looking around the apartment. "The place looks awfully neat."

"Grady snuck in here this afternoon and cleaned the whole apartment."

"As a housewarming gift," he said, red-faced. "It was really for my sake. You know how nuts I get about dust." As if to demonstrate his point, he started polishing his glasses.

Candace saw the look on my face. "He had a spare key back from when Alexandra and Penny lived here."

"I gave it back to Candace," Grady promised me in that charming soft voice of his.

"But . . . how did you get past our watchdog?"

Secretly, I was putting a lot of faith in the idea that old Molly would protect me from any intruders. Grady sneaking into our apartment like that broke the faith in a big way.

"I figured out her schedule," Grady said proudly.

"What schedule?"

"Oh, she's very regular. Twelve to one she's always over at the community garden working on her roses."

"How was Chinese history?" Candace asked me, obviously trying to change the subject.

"Pretty boring."

"Ellie's taking Chinese history," she explained to Grady.

"I don't know if I am going to stick with it or drop it," I said. I still longed for the days of high school when almost everything was decided for you. I didn't know what courses to take, I really didn't. The only

91

reason I was taking Chinese history was because it met at the right time and I needed a fifth course to fill out my schedule.

I dropped my pile of books on the coffee table, which was an old door resting on milk cartons. I flopped down on the sofa. I could feel stuff dropping out of my pockets and idly watched my keys fall down between the cushions.

"Where should we go for dinner?" Grady asked.

I was about to say that I was feeling ravenous and was in the mood for the famous pizza at V&T's restaurant on Amsterdam Avenue. Then I glanced up and saw that Grady was talking to Candace (naturally!) not me. The way he was looking at her, with such naked romantic longing, embarrassed and thrilled me at the same time. It was like I was watching a movie.

"Oh, hey, Candace?" he went on softly. "I forgot to tell you. Stuart and I found this really great vegetarian Chinese place in the Village. You gotta check it out. Everything on the menu is meat, but it's all vegetables." He laughed. "You order steak and you get yams."

"Story of my life," I said.

Candace winked at me.

"The food is great—and cheap," Grady said. "Anyway, I thought we could cab down there and maybe go to the Bottom Line and hear—"

"Grady." She said it gently, but it stopped him. "I thought we settled this."

I started toward my bedroom, but Candace turned quickly, her face pained, and said, "Where are you going?"

"Bathroom," I said.

"Hey, I have an idea," Candace said, faking a brainstorm. "Ellie, why don't you come with us to dinner?"

What a wonderful idea, running interference for Candace. No thank you.

"Oh, no, I couldn't, I already ate."

Candace looked surprised. "You did? Whadya have?"

I know I'm a terrible liar, but it always amazes me how consistently I get caught. "Did I say I ate? I didn't eat, actually, but I'm not feeling well and—"

"Grady wouldn't mind, would you, Grady?"

"No, no, of course not, I—"

"No," I said, with a firmness that surprised me. "But thanks."

Which was when the intercom buzzed. Candace hurried to answer it—hoping for more interference between her and Grady, I guess. She got it.

"It's Stuart," came the garbled voice.

It took a lot to surprise Candace, but now she turned red. "Who?"

"Stuart." And now, just at the wrong time, the intercom cleared itself of static and the next words boomed out loud and clear. "Grady's roommate. Remember? I helped you move in."

"Oh, yeah, Stuart! Come on up!"

She buzzed him in at great length, then left the door open. I glanced at Grady—he looked stunned. I looked away.

"Your roommate," Candace explained as she came back down the entrance hallway. "I guess he knew you were here."

Grady shook his head.

"Oh," Candace said. "Well then, it's just a big coincidence, I guess."

93

Then we all listened in silence to the loud footsteps of Stuart climbing four floors of worn linoleum.

"Candace?"

"You're almost there," Candace called to him.

From where I was standing, I got the first look at him, coming in the door. I saw the big bouquet of roses in one hand and the brown paper bag in the other, an unmistakable bottle shape. Apparently, great roommate minds thought alike.

We all waited as Stuart walked into the apartment, down the long hallway, into the light.

"Wow," he said, "you've got enough books. By the way, you've got a crazy super, you know that? That old woman interrogated me for twenty minutes before she let me buzz—"

He had turned the corner into the living room and was staring at Grady.

"Hi," Grady said glumly.

"Heyyy," Stuart said, his face going through surprise, fear, and then fake happiness very quickly, "I didn't know you were here." Which, I'm sure, was true. He looked down at the flowers and wine he was holding, obviously searching for some explanation. "I just thought you guys needed a housewarming—"

And then his eyes settled on me. And I saw the inspiration hit. "Ellie," he said. "These are for you."

None of us believed him for a second, but as for me, I had fun playing along, and Candace went with the lie in a big way. She'd always been trying to fix me with up with her castoffs. This was a perfect opportunity.

Why did Grady put up with the charade? Probably because he was so discreet and polite. Maybe he figured he'd wait until he got Stuart home and beat him up in private.

94

So first I had to put my bouquet of roses in water (there was no pitcher or vase left for mine, so we had to use the black umbrella stand) and then Stuart uncorked the wine and toasted me. I ended up drinking a whole glass very fast, which, on an empty stomach, had a dizzying effect on me. And then Candace insisted that we *all* go down to Vegetarian Paradise for dinner.

And before I knew what hit me, we were packed in a cab (with Stuart up front with the driver) hurtling down Broadway, bouncing wildly over potholes and driving way too fast.

For me, the fun of having Stuart pretend to be pursuing me began to wear off in the cab. Mainly, I guess, because by then Stuart himself had stopped pretending. He was turned all the way around in his seat, talking straight back at Candace, ignoring the glares from Grady, who was sitting next to me.

"I think we're going too fast," I said. "Aren't we going too fast?"

"Faster?" the cabdriver asked in a heavy foreign accent. And he started driving faster, so that now I felt like we had entered a video game and were dodging the other cars like monsters and at any second we would finally hit one and I would hear that computerized sound of dying as I faded from the screen.

Stuart had brought both bottles of wine (because the vegetarian restaurant didn't have a liquor license) and I had another whole glass before the food came. So now I felt as if I were flying high above New York City. And at the same time the way Stuart and Grady were both fighting for Candace made me sick with a very sober anger and despair.

I made it through the vegetarian moo shu pork and the imitation steamed flounder made out of taro root. But by the time the banana tofu pudding arrived, I stood up to leave, my head whirling.

"I'm just so exhausted," I said. But Candace, who was also pretty drunk by then, grabbed my arm and pulled me back into my seat and pinched me under the table.

"Ow," I said matter-of-factly.

So I didn't get to leave until we were lined up outside the Bottom Line. Grady and Stuart were both arguing with the man in the box office, trying to get him to sell us tickets to a sold-out show. Stuart was pretending—insisting—that he had made reservations, but Grady kept going with the honest decent begging approach, which was messing up Stuart's lie.

"I'm outta here," I told Candace.

"Please," she said in a fierce whisper, "it'll be so awkward if you leave me now, c'mon, give me a break."

"It's awkward *now*," I said, pulling my arm free.

"Okay," she said, "but how are you going to get home?" She looked genuinely concerned, but I was too annoyed with her at the moment to appreciate it.

"I'll take a cab," I said. I said it over my shoulder without looking back. That's a mean thing to do, and the few times in my life that I've done it, I've regretted it. It may sound like a little thing, but it's one of those things that sticks with you. I lie awake some nights—honestly—trying to picture what the look on Candace's face was as I walked across Bleecker Street and left her to an awkward night with two feuding roommates. I think the look was one of surprise, because jumping ship was the kind of thing that Candace would never have done. She would never let down a friend like that. Sure, she was using me that night. Sure, I was in an awful position, which was no position at all. But it was the kind of favor Candace herself would have gladly repaid me a million times over.

Anyway, I got my comeuppance very quickly. I had reached Sixth Avenue and was about to raise my arm to hail one of an endless stream of available cabs when I remembered that I didn't have any money.

I'd spent my last few dollars that afternoon on three used paperback screenplays I'd found on the street. I'd been meaning to hit the ATM for more cash but had forgotten.

A cab slowed down and honked softly, the driver leaning forward to look at me questioningly. I shook my head.

Maybe I should just hail a cab, ride up to school, and then have the cabdriver wait while I went up to the apartment for some money, I thought.

I nixed that idea quickly. I was picturing an angry crazed cabdriver following me up into my apartment, while old Molly slept soundly in the basement.

Now what?

It was no problem, I told myself. But every instinct in my body was screaming *Problem! Problem!*

No problem—I would just go to one of the many ATMs around here and get cash. I didn't like the idea of using an ATM at night, mind you. I'd heard and read plenty of stories of people getting mugged that way. But if I only did it this once, what were the odds I'd have any trouble?

That was Dad's statistics argument, and it was about as effective on me as it was on Mom.

I walked up Sixth, trying to comfort myself with the

streams of people out enjoying the Village artsy-fartsy outdoor café scene. I even stopped to browse at the table of a man selling incense. I was thinking that if I acted like I was as calm as everyone else, maybe I'd feel that way.

Then I saw a large well-lit bank across the street with a crowd of people inside and I really started feeling better.

I crossed the street, got out my bank card, and was about to use it to open the door when the door opened for me.

At my feet sat an old woman wrapped in a beige blanket like an Indian. She was sitting on the dirty butt-strewn floor right inside the door. She had a tattered Dixie cup in her hand with a few coins inside. She was toothless and smelled like she'd gone to the bathroom in her clothes a long time ago. "Some money for a poem?" she asked me.

"I beg your pardon?"

"A few coins for a poem . . ."

I reached in my pocket and found a handful of change, but just then the man at the head of the line started cursing.

"What's the matter?" someone else on line asked.

"It ate my card," the man said.

A groan went up the line, like the wave cheer they did at Columbia football games. People started filing past me.

The old woman was staring at me with gray watery eyes. She shook her cup angrily. But I let the change fall back into my pocket. I might need it.

Out on the street again, I followed the crowd that had surged out of the bank. A number of people were headed for the subway.

The subway.

Few things scared me more than the New York City subway system.

And the New York City subway system *at night* was a whole other story.

On the other hand, it was only nine, and there was such a big crowd headed down the subway steps, how dangerous could it be? Besides, the crowd was carrying me with it. I felt a momentary impulse of bravery.

If I could pull this off . . . if I could ride a New York City subway at night . . . then I'd really be a grown-up. Then I'd really have conquered my fears.

I caught a whiff of a familiar bad smell in the air behind me—something like the bad smell I'd smelled in the bank a few minutes ago.

I ignored it.

I walked down into the dark mouth of the subway.

CHAPTER 14

I DIDN'T HAVE A TOKEN. I HAD TO PUSH ALMOST every bit of change I had—including five pennies— into the smooth wooden slot for the angry-looking woman in the token booth. She counted out my coins laboriously and furiously, then pushed back a single copper-colored token. As I took it I accidentally dropped my last two pennies into the urine-stained dirt at the base of the booth.

I left the pennies. I put my token in the turnstile and went downstairs, deeper underground. I was now totally penniless. That old woman back at the bank had more money than I did.

No problem!

I would take the uptown A train and transfer at Fifty-ninth for the uptown local 1 or 9. I repeated this simple plan over and over to myself like a prayer. As long as I didn't stay on the A (which after Fifty-ninth Street would shoot me right up into the poverty-stricken and terribly dangerous slum neighborhoods that lurked just above Barnard) and as long as I didn't get on the 2 or 3 express (which wouldn't stop at Barnard either but would take me to different parts of those same dangerous neighborhoods) I would be fine.

I would be fine.

The uptown A platform was reassuringly crowded. The train came quickly. And it was only as I was boarding that I saw—way down the platform—the now familiar lumpish figure of the old woman wrapped in the frayed beige blanket, boarding the train at the other end.

Nothing menacing about that, I told myself. When the ATM had broken, business had died for the old woman as well. She was going to be working the subway for a while. She'd probably sleep in one of the cars.

Just an old homeless woman.

I mean, not every old lady was a cause for alarm, right?

The first time I ever went into New York City by myself (to go to a concert at the Beacon Theater with my cousin) my father had given me some nervous instructions. 1) Always take a cab. 2) If for some unforeseen emergency reason you need to take a subway, never ever get on an empty car. 3) If at all possible, sit in the car with the conductor.

After giving me these sound precepts, he'd smiled sickly and said, "You'll be fine," in a way that convinced me I would be dead before the end of the night.

Well, now it was time to apply rule number 2. I made sure I got on a very crowded car.

At least, it was crowded at West Fourth Street. But people kept getting off and few people were getting on, and by the time we had made it to Forty-second and Eighth, I was coming close to breaking rule number 2. I looked over at the closed door to the conductor's control booth. At least I was still obeying rule number 3.

And then I saw the old woman, making her way through the car behind mine. I watched her panhandle for a moment. The train was moving fast, and my car and the car behind me were twisting and turning. So I couldn't always see through the door into the next car. Every time I could see, though, the old woman was closer to the door, closer to my car. . . .

I stood up, ready to bolt off the train. I didn't want to be in the same car with the woman. Irrational, I know. After all, what did the old woman have against me? Would she really kill me because I hadn't given her any change at the bank? Wasn't that as silly as thinking that Arlene the waitress was really Arlene the serial killer because we weren't leaving her big tips?

But I tried to get off the train nevertheless, and would have, too, if the doors hadn't closed right in my face. The rubber edge of the doors chomped down on my arm a couple of times, like a toothless shark trying to gum me to death. Then came the conductor's voice blaring with incredible volume, *"Please step out of the doors, you're holding everyone up."*

I stepped back, the doors slapped closed, and the train lurched forward.

And then the door at the end of my car opened and the old woman came on.

She looked right at me.

I glanced to my left. Then to my right.

In the drama of trying to escape my car, I hadn't noticed how many people had left the car at the last stop. Now I noticed.

As I turned my head wildly I saw nothing but empty seats.

The old woman and I—

We were alone.

CHAPTER 15

THE OLD WOMAN SAT DOWN ACROSS FROM
me, arranging a few tattered paper bags at her feet. I
saw one of those feet. It was bare and yellow, the foot
swollen, the skin cracking open in several places.
"Want to hear a poem?" she asked me.

She doesn't recognize me, I told myself. She
doesn't—

The woman tilted her head back as if for inspiration and started reciting her poem. "There was an old
woman who lived in a shoe. She had so many children
she didn't know what to do."

Her voice was singsong, yet nasty.

"She gave them some broth without any bread.
She whipped them all soundly and put them to bed!"

Her voice rose for the finish. Then she cackled.
And then she got up—moving with a speed that
surprised and alarmed me—and came across the car
toward me.

She shoved her Dixie cup at me. I reached into my
pocket.

Which was empty.

"I'm really sorry," I said, "but I don't have a single penny on me. Honest."

The woman kept studying me with those gray watery eyes of hers. She wasn't holding on to the pole or the overhead bars. When the train rocked, she fell forward, bracing herself with one grimy hand against my shoulder. I smelled her deeply now, smelled her body and her clothes and her breath. Then I squirmed free.

"C'mon," she said. "Give us some change. You asked for a poem."

I hadn't asked for a poem, but I wasn't going to argue the point. I was sweating horribly. "Please," I said. "I'm sorry. I really don't have any money on me. You saw. The bank was broken. Broken," I repeated, as if she didn't understand English.

I was moving away, slowly sliding down the bench, keeping my eyes on her the whole time. But the old woman was moving with me, and now she put a hand out toward me. I don't know what she was planning on doing with that hand, but it was halfway to my throat when I bolted out of the seat. I hurried to the conductor's door, which I'd been eyeing every now and then ever since the old woman entered my car. If things got really bad, I figured I'd knock on that door.

Well, things were getting really bad. The old woman was making her way toward me.

I pounded on the door.

The door was flimsy, with just a small metal latch. When I pounded, it swung open.

The conductor's booth was empty.

CHAPTER 16

THE OLD LADY WAS LAUGHING, A HOARSE awful laugh that was filled with coughs and wheezes. "He's in the other booth," she said, tittering. "The conductor is in the *other* booth."

I was cornered in front of this booth. The old woman reached out and felt my hair. I grabbed her shoulders, my fingers slipping through her blanket and touching bare clammy skin, and held her back as I moved around her. I pulled violently on the door to the next car.

It was locked.

The train screeched against the tracks. The noise sounded like a scream in my ears. Or maybe I was screaming.

And then, only then, I felt the car slowing down beneath my feet. Knowing the station was near gave me the strength to face my attacker. I turned. The old lady was right behind me. She hawked as if she were about to spit at me. I jerked my head backward, banging it against the metal of the door.

Then the conductor's loud voice blasted reassuringly through the car. *"Station stop is Fifty-ninth Street. Fifty-ninth Street."*

The conductor's announcement had a magical effect on the old lady. She went back to a seat and sat down, politely waiting. She didn't even look at me.

"Change here for the number one, the nine, the A, B, C, and D. Please watch your step getting off the train and remember to take your personal belongings with you."

And remember not to ride the New York City subways *ever* *ever* *ever* again.

But I still had one more ride, because I had no money on me now, and besides the old woman had stayed behind me on the A train as I got off. I heard her reciting her poem again—"There was an old woman who lived in a shoe. . . ."—as the doors closed. I could only pray that no one gave her a penny.

The number 1 train was crowded, clean, well lit, with plenty of Columbia and Barnard students—I could pick them out easily. I sat huddled in the corner, my forehead damp with sweat as if I had a fever. I was safe. Safe. The word soothed me like a baby's pacifier. I closed my eyes.

So I almost missed the garbled announcement at Ninety-sixth Street that the train was now running express, and I had to dive off the train, those rubber-edged doors making yet another grab at me. I had just missed another nightmare.

I decided not to wait for the next local. I was jittery from what felt like so many brushes with death. I walked up Broadway, quickening my pace as I went through the dead zone around 106th Street, where the upper West Side stops for a few blocks and the Barnard/Columbia scene has yet to begin.

Then I turned onto our now familiar block, telling myself that the footsteps echoing in my ears were my imagination, not someone following me at all. I looked back a couple of times and saw no one, which was scary enough in itself. Then I started to run.

I made it to the awning of our building. No Molly. Where was that old woman! She was supposed to be outside—always. And now I was sure I heard footsteps, but I was too scared to look.

Another one of my father's rules of New York safety was: Always have your key in your hand as you approach your building. Vestibules of doormanless buildings were not the kind of place you wanted to spend any extra time, especially at night. And tonight for some reason the vestibule of the Boot was pitch-black.

I shoved through the glass door, headed for the locked inner door, my hand already inside my pocket reaching for my key.

Which wasn't there.

And right then my brain did a flash cut—like in a Hitchcock movie I once saw where the serial killer suddenly remembers he dropped a stickpin with his initials on it at the scene of his last murder. Only *I* saw my keys dropping out of my pocket and sliding down between the sofa cushions.

I had only an instant to panic.

Because at that moment two strong hands clapped down on me from behind.

CHAPTER 17

"HEY, HEY, HEY, EASY, EASY, EASY," MY
attacker said as I let out a few strangled screams.

There was a face in my face—a big round moon
face with white scraggly hair. A big figure in the dark,
a woman, in a familiar-looking ratty, baggy, gray
sweater.

"It's Molly, it's Molly," the old woman said, still
holding me.

"Molly," I said. I gulped for air like a drowning
victim.

"Yeah, yeah, it's me, it's me," Molly said.

I slumped against the locked front door.

Molly eyed me, then started to chuckle. "You
scared me, screaming like that. My poor old heart
can't take that kind of thing anymore."

"I . . . scared *you*?"

"I thought you were breaking in, didn't recognize
you, then you start screaming like that. What are you
trying to do? Wake up the whole building?"

"S-sorry."

Molly glared up at the broken bulb. "Now, who is

the jerk who did that?" she asked herself. "This city. They get into everything. We ought to have this front door locked. Safer that way. I've told Mrs. Hayes that a hundred times. But she doesn't listen to old Molly. And I'll tell you why, too. She doesn't want to shell out the coins to put the apartment buzzers outside the building. That's why. That's why."

"I'm sure glad it was you," I said. Then a question wormed its way into my head. "W-what were you doing outside so late, anyway?"

She looked back at me steadily.

"Patrolling."

"Huh?"

"At night sometimes I walk up and down the block, down to Broadway and back. Then down to Amsterdam and back. Then back to Broadway—"

I had the idea, but once Molly got started telling you something, there was no stopping her.

"—then back to the building. Then I walk Bert and so I do the laps all over again. It's a lot of work but I got to make sure my children are all home in bed and sleeping safe, right?" She grinned. "Well, no use standing around in the dark. C'mon, open the door."

I turned to face the door, then remembered. "I can't," I said. And then, like a little child who has lost her doll, I suddenly felt the evening become too much for me and I started to cry. "I didn't . . . bring my key," I sobbed.

I was aware even as I cried that this sounded like a ridiculous reason to be crying, but old Molly didn't seem to judge me. She just held out her arms like a polar bear standing on its hind legs and clasped me to her soft chest in a long hug.

110

"There, there," she said. She rocked me in the dark. "It's okay, it's okay."

"It's not. I'm such a baby. And I'm so scared all the time. I can't . . . handle this. I can't handle *anything*."

Molly kept rocking me. "So many children," she mumbled to herself, "don't know what to do."

I felt better soon. Molly pulled out a big metal ring of keys and opened the door, pushing it open ahead of me.

"Thank you," I said, my head down, wiping at the tears with the heel of my hand. "I'm okay now. You caught me at a bad time. I don't want you to think I'm a total mental case or something. I mean, I am, I guess, but— Anyway. Thank you."

Molly grinned at me. "Anytime. Like I told you, I'm always here for you girls. You're my children. And you know something? You're the only children old Molly's got."

"That's nice—very nice of you."

We stood there awkwardly; I didn't know how to make my good-bye. "Well—thank you again." I started up the stairs. Then stopped. I looked down at Molly. "Oh, God. I can't get into my apartment either," I said. "I'm locked out."

"No problem," Molly said with a smile. "I've got the keys to your place down in the basement."

This scared me all over again. "You do?"

"Sure. I've got every apartment. I'm the super, remember?" She chuckled some more. "C'mon."

In Englewood, I was terrified of going down to the basement by myself. I didn't want to go down into this basement either, not now. "Don't you have the key on that big thing of keys?"

"Nope. Got 'em in the basement."

She reached a meaty hand up the stairs toward me. I took it, let her lead me back down.

I had never even looked to see where the entrance to the basement was, nor wondered. Now I followed Molly down the narrow hallway that led to the entrance doors to the first-floor apartments. Under the first-floor stairs there was another flight of stairs leading down.

These were steps of stone.

"Go ahead," Molly said, giving me a little push. "I'm right behind you."

I went down.

"If I could get my hands on the scum who broke that bulb," Molly muttered behind me. "Probably some homeless drunk. Like Fred, that bastard."

"Fred?"

"Don't ask."

I didn't.

"I gotta fix that bulb," she said to herself. "I'll fix it right after I let you into your place. And then I gotta walk Bert. And then I gotta . . ."

I smiled. She was muttering her entire schedule to herself, comforting herself with it. It was the kind of monologue I often had running in my own head, only I never said mine aloud.

The basement smelled of garbage. I saw, by the light of a naked bulb, the boiler, the large trash incinerator, and then—with Molly tugging on my elbow to guide me—I came to the dented brown metal door to her basement apartment.

"Right in here," she said.

She unlocked the door for me. I heard a low growl.

"Don't worry," she said. "He's harmless. Shut up, Bert," she snapped through the door. The whine rose into a question mark, then ceased. Molly opened the door, reached around to flick on the light.

The dog was a big old German shepherd with a red bandanna around his neck. He was swaybacked and had such a depressed manner that I wondered if he had been beaten. Molly patted him gently, though, then ordered him back inside.

Though Molly was basically clean and neat in appearance, I was expecting a mess of an apartment, as if a basement apartment couldn't possibly be neat. The room was small, a shoebox of an apartment, but immaculately clean, with everything positioned just so. The old magazines on the coffee table lay in a neat pile, their edges perfectly straightened. The lamp next to the sofa sat on a white doily. The bathroom door was open. I could see the gleaming faucet and spigot, spotless. And on the wall by the door was a neatly handprinted schedule.

Monday, twelve to one—roses.

One to two—sweep.

"You're on a tight schedule, I see," I said with a smile.

"Oh, yeah. Gotta keep organized, gotta keep organized." She bustled around, turning on lights. "Sit, sit," she said to me.

I sat on the fancy leather sofa.

"You've got a nice place," I said, trying to keep the surprise out of my voice.

"Thank you." She waved her hand around. "Most of the stuff in here is gifts from you students," she said.

"Gifts?"

"Well, not gifts on purpose, gifts you all threw out." She tossed off a bark of a laugh. "The stairs is

113

pretty narrow, as you know. So a lot of tenants leave stuff behind when they move out, and then I pull it down here. That sofa you're sitting on, it belonged to a Barnard girl sixteen years ago."

"Ah."

There was long mantellike shelf with two small artifacts—a tiny shell and a bud vase—each item spaced perfectly across the shelf as if Molly had measured with a ruler.

Molly saw me looking and came over to show me. "I call this my museum."

"Your museum?"

"It's Molly's museum of friendship. These things. They don't look like much, do they?"

"No, they do, they're nice—"

"They're not much, but these are the things my young Barnard children have given to Molly through the years."

That was it? Two presents? I felt a spasm of guilt.

The guilt didn't last long. Because Molly added, "Two special friends . . ."

Special friends. And who might those special friends be? The names that went through my head made my hair stand on end—Leiter, Sanchez, Silver.

And then came another word. A word from that fax Candace had read in the police station.

Souvenirs.

The killer was keeping mementos.

I had been picturing body parts or skulls, something grisly. But maybe the souvenirs were nice things, like that tiny shell and that vase.

But there were only two gifts. Two gifts, three girls.

"This shell was from a girl named Patsy Potter. That's a funny name, isn't it? She lived in 2-B. She was so afraid of the dark that I had to sing to her some nights to help her go to sleep. She missed her mommy. And wouldn't you know? That girl became a brain surgeon? She came by once to see me. Came by to see old Molly. She says, 'Molly, I just want you to know, it was you who got me through college. You were my savior.'"

Molly had gotten a little teary. She put the shell back down.

I felt another wave of guilt. Here I was suspecting the poor old woman of murder.

Molly filled a plastic water bowl for the dog, who lapped it furiously. She patted his head again. Another thing I was wrong about, I told myself. I had thought that she beat him. Instead, the dog's timidity must have come from being locked up down here in the basement. Though I did think it was strange that I'd never seen him outside with Molly for a walk.

But my logical mind came up with the solution for that quickly. Molly kept to a rigid schedule. I was on a regular schedule myself, what with my course load. So if Bert's walks overlapped with my courses, I would never see him.

"I never knew you had a dog," I said.

"Oh, yeah," she said, stroking him gently. "Poor Bert. I found him on the street. Someone beat the crap out of him. Scared him good. Took the fight out of him. He's not much of a guard dog. It's more like old Molly has to guard him." She laughed.

I silently lacerated myself for thinking the worst of her once more.

"I can't even let him run around in the park off his leash," she said. "He gets so sad and scared he just falls to the ground shaking. Right, Bert? You only feel safe when you're down here with old Molly."

I gave myself another twenty lashes.

Molly came toward me. "See this?"

She shoved her fist at me so quickly I ducked back as if she were trying to punch me.

"Easy now, easy now," she cooed. "You scare easy, don'tcha?"

"Yes, I do. But I've also had a kind of a harrowing night."

"Well, don't worry, Molly'll fix you something warm to drink and you'll tell me all about it and then you'll feel different, I promise you."

She was still holding her wrist out to me. "Look," she commanded.

She was showing me, I finally realized, her watch. It was a Swatch watch with a green band. The watch face showed a golfer taking a swing. A little golf ball was traveling around on the second hand, so that once a minute it looked like the golfer was teeing off.

"Girl in 3-C left it on a nail in the bathroom last year," Molly said. "Keeps perfect time, too. Which is good, because I got to keep to my schedule. I got so much to do."

She looked off into space, her lips moving; I guessed that she was repeating her schedule to herself again. Even though I felt bad for having misjudged her, I felt a strong impulse to get out of there. The room was windowless; the ceiling was low. I could feel the weight of the whole building pressing down on us from above. If the building was indeed a shoe, then

116

we were in the heel, and the building was trying to grind us into dust.

"Now," she said, moving to the small kitchenette, "what can I get you?"

"Oh, nothing—nothing at all, I'm sorry to have troubled you so much already. If you could just give me the keys—" I started to get up, but she fixed me with a commanding look that made me sit back down again.

"What can I get you?" she repeated.

Good manners were deeply ingrained in me throughout childhood. I couldn't fight them for long, not even when I was sitting in a tiny basement apartment all alone with the odd, old super late at night. "Well," I said, "if you have a glass of water . . ."

"I'll make you my specialty. Chicken broth. You know," Molly said, opening the fridge, "they've done studies. Science studies. Shows this chicken broth is good for colds."

"I don't have a cold," I said.

"Well, this will keep you from getting one."

The dog was excited by the opening of the fridge. Molly shooed him away with her foot. "Not for you, Bert," she said.

She put a small saucepan under the tap; the water drilled into it. "So tell me what happened," she said.

"What do you mean?"

"You said you had a bad night."

"Oh, yes, I did, well, I don't want to burden you."

Molly checked the flame on the stove, then scratched her face roughly. She sat down across from me in a big old rocker.

"Eleanor," she said.

It shocked me, hearing my full name like that,

117

especially since only my mother ever called me that. It took me a second before I remembered that that was what I had told Molly my name was, the first time I had met her.

"Yes?"

"Look around," she said.

Dutifully, I looked.

"See anybody?"

"No."

"I'm all alone down here. Got nothing to do. I like hearing my children's problems, believe me. It makes old Molly feel better if I can help."

"Well," I said. I took a breath. "It started when I came home tonight and Grady—"

I stopped short. First of all, I felt half-insane telling this old woman my troubles. Secondly, I had remembered how Molly felt about boys being in the building.

She hadn't missed my slip. "I don't like them boys buzzing around Candace," she said darkly. "I tried to keep that one out tonight, that tall one, but he kept saying he was invited."

"He wasn't," I blurted out. "But we know him. I mean, it's okay."

Molly rocked. "It's not okay. You never know what a boy will try. Especially that one. The other one is okay, he's clean and tidy. But that one. He's got slime all over him."

I laughed. She had a point.

"I don't like that slimy one hanging around Candace."

"Candace can handle herself, believe me."

Molly nodded. "Yeah, that's right. Candace can handle herself. So can old Molly. And so can you. That's what we women have to remember, right?

118

We don't have to lean on men. We can stand up for ourselves."

I could see why Candace liked Molly so much.

The Columbia mascot was a lion; for Barnard it was a bear. They could have almost used old Molly as the mascot instead. I pictured the campus's main gates. Instead of the little metal bear that stood in a small circle above the entrance, they could put a statue of old Molly holding her broom like a weapon.

Barnard was one of the few all-women schools left in the country. Going here was supposed to teach you pride and confidence in yourself as a woman. Old Molly was preaching the school song.

"So what about you?" I asked. "You never, uh, married?"

Molly had gotten out of the rocker and was on her way to the stove. She turned around, her face cloudy with anger. "Why do you ask me that?"

"I—I don't know, I just—I'm sorry."

"No, no, no, there's nothing wrong with asking." She stirred the broth. "It just makes me so mad sometimes when I think about—"

The steam from the broth swirled up into her face.

"Every man I ever been with stabbed me in the back, one way or another. Until I learned never to trust them no more.

"So no," she said finally. "I never been married. Never will be married."

"Oh, now," I said, sounding like my mother, "never say never."

"Never."

We both laughed.

"I mean, who would marry a fat old broad like me?"

"You can't have that attitude," I said. "You can't think negatively."

"Why? You do."

She had me there.

"What about you?" she asked. "Still no boyfriends?" She was inspecting her spice rack. She sprinkled something white into the saucepan.

"No," I said. "Sometimes I feel like I never will."

Molly gave me a serious look. "Keep it that way. You'll live longer."

I nodded.

"You gotta watch out, though. You're a pretty girl, Ellie."

"I wish."

"You are. And when you believe it about yourself, then the boys will start noticing it, and then they'll come lapping around like a bunch of wild hounds and man oh man that's when the trouble starts. You hear me? So watch yourself."

Just then, as if trying to prove Molly's point—not just that I would get attention but also that men were like wild dogs—the German shepherd slouched over to me and tried to shove his long sad snout into my lap.

"Bert," Molly warned him. The dog slunk off, thumping his tail against the cold cement floor; he did three or four laps around his blanket, then finally settled back down.

Molly was looking in her cupboards. "I'd give you some crackers with this, but it don't look like I got any. How about some bread?"

"No, that's okay, really I—"

She opened the fridge. "No bread."

Molly poured the broth into a Styrofoam cup.

"Here," she said. She handed it to me. I took it with both hands.

The steam rising from the cup smelled wonderful.

I actually wished Molly had found some crackers. When I was growing up, my mother always seemed to be depressed; usually I had to take care of her instead of the other way around, trying to cheer her up, entertain her, listen to her problems, stuff like that. The one time I felt like I really got mothered was when I was sick. Mom would bring me my meals in bed on a tray, chicken soup with Ritz crackers that she'd crumble into the soup for me. The smell of the broth took me back to those feverish days and nights. The soup smelled like mother love itself.

"Drink," Molly told me.

I lifted the cup to my lips. . . .

CHAPTER 18

THERE WAS A KNOCK AT THE DOOR.

"Molly?"

I started so badly I sloshed some broth onto my hand, burning myself. Then I set the cup down on the coffee table so quickly that I spilled some more. The knocking at the door continued as Molly hurried to get a washrag to wipe the spill and as I apologized profusely.

Then Molly opened the door and let in—

"Hi," Candace said, "I'm really sorry to bother you so late, I hope I'm not waking you up, but I managed to lock myself out of—"

She saw me, her jaw dropped. "There you are." There was relief in her face.

"Hi."

"I was really worried about you. I figured you'd be home for sure by now. I already called the cops."

"You did?"

I felt so grateful to her for worrying about me that I wanted to cry. Again.

Molly laughed. "Look at the two of you. Two roommates, neither one of you has the sense to bring their keys with them."

She shook her head as she unlocked a plain plywood chest that hung on the wall. Inside was a peg rack dangling with labeled keys. "Four-B, right?"

We followed her out of the apartment, with Bert whining behind the door as Molly closed and locked it behind us. Then we had to follow her up the stairs. I felt bad about making her climb four flights, wheezing and stopping to rest at every stairwell, helping herself up and around the corners by pushing down on the newel posts with her beefy hand. I kept apologizing. She kept insisting she was glad to do it.

It wasn't until after she had let us into the apartment and was heading back down the stairs that I remembered the soup. I hadn't even tasted it.

"Another time," Molly promised.

That night Candace and I stayed up talking for hours. We lay on our backs in her bed in the dark, bouncing our thoughts off the ceiling. Finally, around two, our conversation began to wind down into long peaceful silences.

"So you've forgiven me, right?" I asked.

"For what?"

"For tonight, for running off."

"Ellie—"

Candace always had to remind me that she didn't hold grudges. I found it hard to believe. I came from a house where harsh words were treasured as sore memories for years. But it was true with Candace; she got angry and then it was gone.

"And also," I said, "for getting so mad that other time, about Jenny and everything."

"Oh, that," Candace said. "Now that I haven't forgiven you for."

We both laughed. I rolled over, my head resting on Candace's hand. Her mermaid ring was hard against my cheek. I sat up. "Let me try on that ring."

"No."

I was shocked. Candace and I shared all our clothes, borrowing things from each other's closets whenever we wanted.

"Why not?"

"Because it won't come off."

"Get out."

I pulled on the ring, but she was telling the truth; it was stuck tight.

Once again I had misjudged her. Not lending Candace something, on a momentary whim, that was something I might do, not Candace.

"Candace?"

"What?"

"Why I can't be like you?"

"I don't know. Why would you want to be?"

"Oh, for about a million reasons."

"Like?"

"Like . . . I'd love to be independent like you."

"Sometimes I think I'm too independent."

"What do you mean?"

A siren sounded in the distance, part of the city's nightly lullaby.

"I can't imagine ever falling in love, for one thing," Candace said. "The thought of being dependent on someone gives me the creeps."

124

"All right," I said, "maybe you are too independent. But why can't I be a little like you?"

"Because you weren't raised like me. I have two loudmouth overconfident parents and three loudmouth overconfident older brothers and I was taught from, well, in utero basically, that I can do anything I want to do in this world. You were taught the opposite."

"It's true," I said mournfully. "So what am I going to do about it?"

"Go to Ruth."

"That sounds like a curse."

"I couldn't live without her."

Ruth Golden was one of the shrinks that Barnard provided to their students free of charge. Candace had gone all freshman year. She was going again this year, too.

"I just can't get my mind around that, that you go to a shrink," I said.

"Why?"

Abby was another one of Ruth's patients. That made sense to me. But Candace?

"I've never known anyone who needed a shrink less than you."

"That's because I've been going for ten years. Everyone in my family goes. And then we go to family therapy. And my parents go to couples therapy. This is Manhattan, Ellie. If you don't go to a shrink, you're a freak."

"I'm a freak."

"Ellie?"

"What?"

"Would you say you're happy?"

"No."

"Take a minute to think about it, why don'tcha?"

Candace laughed. Then she sat up and gazed down at me in the dark.

"Do me a favor," she said. "Just try it. One session. That's all I ask. I'm begging you, Ellie, and I don't like to beg. One session, Ellie. Tell it to Ruth."

One of the main reasons I had never gone to a shrink was that I was worried I needed therapy too much. It was like the time I thought I was having a heart attack. I was having these chest pains. At the time Abby and I were hanging out at this new Mexican restaurant, Pancho Villa, having late-night nachos all the time. (It was Abby's idea. Abby had the world's worst eating habits.)

Later that night I'd get these horrible stabs right in the heart. There was no way I was going to see a doctor, though, because I figured the doctor would tell me I was having a heart attack and then I would die. Somehow it seemed to my mature mind that if I avoided the doctor then I wouldn't die.

Of course, when I finally confessed the whole thing to Candace, she laughed and explained that I had heartburn and should stop eating nachos with Abby late at night.

It was the same with shrinks. I was terrified that a shrink would listen to my problems and institutionalize me on the spot. If I didn't go to a shrink, then I wasn't crazy.

There was another reason I was reluctant. At Barnard, the shrinks' offices were on the same floor as some of the main classrooms and lecture halls. So everyone saw you going for your appointment. Everyone knew you were nuts.

But at this point I was desperate. I called and made the appointment the next morning. And that Thursday at quarter to four I headed over to campus.

I don't know if you've ever been to Barnard. I hadn't before I went there. My parents wanted to drive all over the country with me checking out schools, but I couldn't bear the thought of it. So I just sent away for some catalogs and filled out my applications (the night before the deadline and two months after my mother and father had two nervous breakdowns apiece). I was shocked the first time I saw Barnard's main buildings.

For one thing, the school is the size of a postage stamp. Especially when you compare it with the gigundo Columbia campus right across the street. For another, there's nothing special looking or even college looking about a lot of the buildings, especially on the inside. Maybe I had too many fantasies about what college would be like. But most of the buildings looked just like run-down public high schools.

The elevator to the third floor was brown and beat-up and rickety, like you'd expect to find in crazy Esther Green's old apartment building. Every time I was in the elevator I felt I was taking my life in my hands.

I didn't run into anyone on the way to Ruth Golden's office. You see, Ellie. Not so bad as you thought.

Which was always the way, I reminded myself.

Everything I worried and worried about always turned out to be No Big Deal.

The door to Ruth's office had a manila envelope taped out front with her name on it, just like a teacher's office. I knocked.

"Come in," said a voice with a heavy Russian accent.

I turned the knob. The door was locked. Either that or I was such a weakling that I couldn't open the door.

I started to sweat. What a way to start my very first shrink session ever! I turned the knob harder. But now my palm was so sweaty I couldn't get a grip on the doorknob.

"Oh, sorry," I heard Ruth say. "I forgot I locked—"

And then the door flew open.

And I was face-to-face with the old woman.

CHAPTER 19

"SORRY, SORRY, SORRY," RUTH SAID, "I'M getting so senile it's really a horror movie. Come in, come in. My my, you look like a frightened little bunny rabbit." She chuckled. "I'm so sorry. Did I startle you with that door business? Oh, what a way to begin, eh? Well, sit, sit, please, please."

There was a desk with a leather chair behind it, and in front of that was another leather chair, but that chair was turned to face the sofa.

"Where do I . . . ?"

"Oh, on the sofa, but you don't have to lie down or anything like that, I'm not Dr. Freud, ha-ha."

I sat.

"Now, you are Ellie Sommers, Candace's roommate, correct?"

"Yes."

"Good, good, so you see, I'm not totally losing all the marbles, as they say. Care for a cookie? They're homemade."

"Oh, no thank you."

"Why not? Peanut butter. Delicious. If I must say

so myself. Okay. I leave them here on the desk if you want one." She folded two small wrinkled hands in her lap and looked at me kindly.

Ruth Golden was little and spry with salt-and-pepper hair that she wore tucked in a neat bun. She had a sloped back, like old women sometimes get, and it made her lean forward a little, as if she were always asking, "Yes?" Today she was wearing a dark cotton skirt and a purple blouse the color of eggplant.

But I'm not describing her well at all; I'm not getting to the heart of it. Candace had always told me there was something magical about Ruth, and I felt it, too—she was like a good witch.

"Okay," she said.

"Okay what?" I asked, clearing my throat.

"Why don't you tell me a little about yourself, some basic facts, or wherever you want to start. Something that's bothering you lately, a dream, anything at all."

I took a deep breath. "I've never done this before."

"What, therapy? Oh, well, there's a first time for everything." She smiled.

"Well," I said. "I'm very upset about that girl, Jenny Silver, who's missing."

Ruth nodded. "Yes, yes, that is very frightening business. She is my patient, you know."

"She is? Oh, I didn't know that."

I blushed. I thought shrinks were supposed to keep strict confidentiality about everything you discussed with them. Would Jenny have wanted me to know that she was in therapy? Would I want anyone else to know that I was in therapy? No way.

But Candace had told me that Ruth was very unconventional. I guessed this was part of it.

"I hope they find her soon," I said.

"So do I, so do I, so do I."

She said this so sincerely and so warmly that I forgave her for the slip about Jenny.

"Do you know her?" she asked me.

"A little."

Ruth nodded. "So what are you feeling about her?"

"Scared."

"You look tired. Have you been sleeping good?" She pronounced *good* like *goot* and it took me a moment to decipher it.

"I was for a while, sleeping really well, actually, but lately—"

"Lately?"

"I've been having nightmares."

Another nod. "Do you remember any of these dreams?"

"Yeah. It's always the same. I'm walking around Manhattan at night and then I make a stupid mistake and I find myself in this really bad neighborhood. Burned-out buildings and drug dealers. And then there are these tough kids after me, with sticks and knives or whatever. And I try to run, but it's like I'm moving slower and slower."

"And then?"

"And then I wake up drenched in sweat and gasping for breath and have to say, 'Nightmare, nightmare,' out loud before I can calm down."

"Listen, Ellie, it makes perfect sense you are scared. Of this Jenny Silver case everyone is scared, believe me."

"Does it? Make sense? I feel so scared all the time,

131

I mean, it's almost crippling in a way. Well, not crippling, I don't mean to exaggerate how neurotic I am. I actually have this fear—it's pretty silly, ha-ha—that if I ever went and talked to a shrink, then they would commit me, ha-ha-ha."

"So you are mostly scared right now about Jenny?"

"Jenny, yes. And . . . everything else basically."

"Such as?"

I had thought I wouldn't be able to open up to some stranger. Now it felt more like I was up against the opposite problem. My feelings, my neuroses, my worries—they all seemed to be brimming right below the surface ready to overflow if I opened my mouth.

"I'm worried about my mom," I said.

I didn't expect to say that. And I didn't expect to start crying as soon as I said it. But I did.

Ruth handed me a Kleenex box. I blew my nose. After I had cried for a few minutes, she said gently, "Why are you worried about your mom?"

"Well, because she's so worried about me," I said, crying some more.

"Ah," Ruth said gently. "So you are worried because she is worried? Sounds like we have a worry contest on our hands."

I laughed.

"Tell me about your mother please."

I talked about her for almost the whole session. How it sometimes felt to me like we were the same person. Two frightened little women. When I was in high school I used to get Mom to write excuses for me, saying I was sick when I was just feeling anxious or sad. I'd stay home with her, because she was almost always home as well, and the two of us would mope around the big old house, watching old black-and-white movies on TV, playing the mindless card games of my childhood like casino and spit. They were miserable days, actually, but when I thought of them it was with a painful nostalgia. As if I missed being miserable with Mom.

"I miss her," I said, "even though I can't stand being with her. And I worry about her, too, about her getting old, anything happening to her. That's one of the things that scares me with this whole Jenny business," I said. "I just keep thinking, what would happen if I actually did get killed?"

"God forbid," said Ruth.

"But Mom—it would kill her."

"That's what scares you about dying? That it would upset your mom?"

"I know that sounds silly, but that's a big part of it, yeah. I feel like it would be so humiliating, to be killed, I mean."

"Humiliating? That's an odd description of death, wouldn't you say?"

"No, I don't think so. Especially after my mom has warned me so many times to leave school. If I got killed, that would be like the biggest I-told-you-so of all time."

I blew my nose again.

"Ellie—"

"Yes."

"Jenny Silver has disappeared. We hope she is okay. But let's say she was kidnapped. Does that mean she has done something wrong? She is the victim here, Ellie. And you, I have a feeling, you also are a victim of a mother who has burdened you with some of her own fears, no?"

I nodded. "You know, Dr. Golden—"

"Oh, I'm not a doctor. I'm only a social worker. Just call me Ruth."

"Ruth," I began. I smiled. "Wow, that's hard for me to say. I was taught to be very polite, but anyway, I'll get the hang of it, right? Uh, this whole Jenny thing, it's just the worst possible timing for me. I mean, it's a joke really. Here I've been trying to get myself not to be so fearful of everything all the time. So what happens? A serial killer starts stalking the campus."

"Yes, but," Ruth said. She leaned forward and pointed an arthritic finger at me. "I'm sorry to say this, but of this it's right to be fearful. Don't ever forget this. I don't want to scare you, Ellie, when you already are having nightmares and all this. But you must be careful."

"So everyone keeps telling me."

"I am serious," Ruth repeated. "Be careful. Be as careful as you can. And now"—she reached for her date book—"let's see if we can get organized here and find a regular time for you in our schedule, yes?"

"You cried? In your first session?"

"Yeah, why, is that bad?"

Abby shook her head. "No, it's really good. I'm jealous. It shows you're really trusting."

"I know, that's my problem, I'm way too trusting."

"No such thing."

We were sitting in Abby's little single in Plimpton, an ugly concrete-walled closet of a room that Abby had yet to decorate with a single poster. I had walked straight here after my session, in part as a way of testing out my new bravery. Normally I didn't like to go to Plimpton even by day. But it had felt so good to get out some of that fear, blab it all to Ruth; maybe now I was cured.

"You don't cry in your sessions?" I asked.

"Are you kidding? I cry on my way to the sessions."

"So what are you jealous of?"

Abby didn't answer, just kept cracking more roasted peanut shells and shoving the nuts in her mouth.

"Those are really fattening, by the way," I said.

"That's why I eat them," she said. "I can't believe Candace finally got you to go. How come my begging you to go never had any effect?"

"Abby," I said, "please don't turn this into a contest, too."

"Everything's a contest. And I always lose."

"Hey," I said. "I brought you something."

I pulled out another pepper pen.

"Oh wow," Abby said, when I explained what it was. Her eyes welled with quick tears. "Thanks."

I had a feeling that, like Molly, Abby didn't get presents too often. I made a mental note to buy her a poster for her walls. And maybe I'd buy something for old Molly as well. One therapy session, and here I was turning into Santa Claus.

Abby pulled a book off her desk. "I'm totally lost on that set-theory problem about the apples and the oranges."

"Really? You can't get that one?"

"Hey," Abby said. "I told you from day one. I'm not a logical person. I can't even figure out why I let you talk me into taking the class in the first place."

I laughed. I studied the problem over her shoulder.

I don't want to brag, but while I explained the solution to her I let my mind wander. Promise me you will buy her that poster, I ordered myself. And then I thought about which movie poster I would buy.

I kept my promise.

I bought a poster for Abby.

Only it took me two months before I got around to it.

I was one day too late.

CHAPTER 20

THE PLEASANT SEASONS GO FAST IN Manhattan; spring and fall are little blips on the screen compared with the endless summer and winter. By October, fall weather was already a thing of the past. And by November the streets were lined with ice and the skies were permanently gray, matching the sooty facades of the buildings below.

Jenny Silver had not only physically disappeared, but for many of us, she was now passing from our thoughts as well. Whole weeks went by when I didn't think about her. She was no longer the sole topic of every cafeteria discussion. Even Candace—the most stubborn, persistent person I'd ever met—talked about Jenny less often, and held fewer meetings of her Find Jenny club.

I was going to Ruth Golden twice a week now. I lived for my sessions. I spent my off days thinking about what I had said, what Ruth had said, what I would say. Sometimes I felt like I was making no progress in therapy, but on the other hand, I saw progress in my life. I wasn't so worried these days by serial killers or robbers or bogeymen, or any of the other myriad demons I usually feared.

And then, I had my *other* therapist. I had gotten over my fears of old Molly and had joined the legions of Barnard girls who considered Molly their extra grandmother and friend. She'd adopted us and we'd adopted her. And when I was feeling low, I'd buy lunch and go to the community garden—in a converted old lot on Amsterdam Avenue—and chat with her while she worked on her famous rose bushes. There were no roses this time of year, of course. But she was always sprinkling ash into the beds, which she said prevented something called dieback.

Actually I figured she came to the garden because it was on her schedule, and her schedule was the thing that kept her demons away.

She'd begun to tell me a little about those demons. She'd been raised in a tiny apartment in Queens, one of seven children. Abandoned by their father. So her hatred of men had started early.

Her poor overwhelmed mother had snapped under the strain. "She used to tell us to be good," Molly told me one day in the garden while I stuffed tuna on a bagel into my face. "And when we were bad—"

She swiped her hand through the air, spraying a little dirt from her garden trowel.

"She'd *whip* you?"

"Oh yeah. With a belt."

"Oh, Molly, that's horrible. And I thought I had it rough."

"Well," she said thoughtfully, "everybody has it rough in their own way. That's what I figure.

138

Women, anyway. Men have it easy. See that man over there?"

She pointed with the trowel. There were several concrete tables in the garden with checkerboards built into the tops. When the weather permitted there were flocks of old men like pigeons clustered around those tables, playing chess and checkers and dominoes—and drinking.

"See the tall man with the long silver hair?"

"With the raincoat?"

"To the left. Big beard."

I saw who she meant. He was bony, wild-eyed. Molly spat, then went back to work on her roses, training a scraggly vine back over the weather-beaten wooden trellis. "That's Fred," she said.

"Fred? Your friend?"

"My enemy."

"Why?"

Molly grunted and worked her way back to her feet. She wiped her hands on her overalls. "He's always trying to seduce me."

The thought of someone seducing Molly—it was all I could do to keep the smile off my face.

"Why don't you let him?"

"That's being bad."

"Hey," I said, "your mom's not around to whip you anymore. It's okay."

"No," she said. "Don't trust men, I told you. This summer, when Fred came back? I hadn't seen him for two years. He goes off on these benders of his . . . you never know if he'll come back again."

I had to admit, Fred didn't sound like promising marriage material.

"What about you?" Molly asked.

"What about me what?"

"Boys."

This was another good thing about Molly. With someone like Abby, I always ended up talking about *her* problems the whole time. Candace was often too busy to talk or off at some meeting or other. Molly always asked about me.

"Nothing," I said.

"Good."

I laughed, though I knew she was serious.

"What about that neat one, with the glasses?" she asked.

"Grady? He doesn't come by anymore."

"I know. Why not?"

"I guess he finally realized Candace won't go out with him."

"Good." She searched my face. "What about you? Why doesn't he come asking for you?"

"Oh, well, some guy who's interested in Candace isn't going to settle for me."

She watched me for a second more, as if trying to make sure I was telling the truth. She looked relieved. "Good, good, good."

My misery was her happiness, at least in the boys department.

"What about your major? You sticking with English?"

"Yeah. Which is stupid, I know. I'll never make a living writing. I probably won't publish a single word."

Molly wiped her mouth with the back of one large paw-hand, leaving a smear of dirt. "That's enough of that, Eleanor," she said. "You keep coming to this garden telling old Molly stuff like that, running yourself down. That's enough, now. You hear me? Be proud of yourself. That's it. I told you."

In her own way, Molly complemented therapy beautifully. Therapists were supposed to ask questions, probe gently, get you to realize things for yourself. Old Molly just ordered you to feel better, and sometimes it worked.

Molly checked her Swatch watch. "Well, I gotta go sweep."

I watched her trundle out through the garden's open gates, back out into the noise and traffic of Amsterdam Avenue. She glanced once in Fred's direction, but he didn't look up.

I stayed behind, finishing my sandwich next to the little fat cherub statue, and feeling . . . fine. Doesn't sound like too much of a moment, perhaps. But I'd always had trouble just being by myself and not daydreaming or worrying or disconnecting. Just hanging out. Just being. It was a hard stunt for me.

But right then, with Molly's advice still ringing in my ears, I did it. And I felt a surge of hope for the future.

I couldn't report such great progress or hope for my mother's mental state, however. Even though Jenny hadn't been in the news for a while, it was getting harder and harder to reassure Mom that the campus was safe. And while I felt more comfortable with each passing day, my mother seemed to feel more and more afraid. As she pointed out almost every time she called, each passing day made it less and less likely that Jenny Silver would ever be found. Alive, anyway.

And then, just when I thought maybe my mom had

141

let the subject drop, *Newsweek* ran an article entitled "Stalking the Ivy League," all about the three missing-persons cases.

That night I was on the phone with Mom for two hours straight.

"No wonder you don't have a boyfriend," Candace said to me when I finally hung up.

"What are you talking about?"

"You're on the phone with your mom every second, how could you have time for a social life?"

"She's worried," I said lamely. "What am I supposed to do?"

The phone rang. Candace arched one dark eyebrow, daring me not to answer. I answered. And talked to my mom for another hour.

She sounded so depressed and scared, I was in tears by the time I hung up.

"Crybaby," Candace said mildly as she walked through the living room with her watering can on her way to the sink.

"Shut up," I said.

I called my mother back.

"Oh, that's a terrific idea," Candace said as she headed back to her room.

My father answered, that familiar worried voice.

"Dad? Is she okay?" I asked.

"She's fine, Ellie," he said. He was using his math-professor voice. He *was* a professor, but he only sounded like one when he wanted to get all stuffy and distant.

"She doesn't sound fine," I said.

"Well," he said. "She worries about you, you know."

"So then it's my fault."

142

"Ellie," he said. "Don't make me crazy."

Great. Now I was making him crazy, not just Mom.

"Ruth thinks Mom and you both worry about me so much as a way of avoiding stuff that's going on in your own lives," I said.

There was a heavy pained silence during which I punched my thigh several times as hard as I could. Every time I quoted Ruth to them, I regretted it.

"Well," he said sadly, "that's probably true."

Dad, I wish you hadn't said that, I thought.

Then, as we always did whenever we spoke, we talked about Birnbaum and set theory and how I was doing in that class and whether or not I was thinking about switching to math as a major. But it was as if he were forcing himself to ask these questions, as if he had lost interest in these topics. And when he got off the phone he didn't even ask me to come home and visit soon, which was usually a constant refrain with him.

The next night when I called, he answered again and said my mother was in the shower.

The night after that she was asleep.

"Dad," I said, "what is it? She's not speaking to me?"

"No, no, no."

"And how come you don't ask me to come home and visit anymore. Not that I can come and visit right now, but I still like to be asked."

He didn't even answer. Just sighed.

The next night he said that Mom had gone to the movies with her friend Joan. Joan was Mom's only friend, basically, and they weren't even close. Half the time they weren't speaking to each other. The idea of them going to the movies together sounded ludicrously farfetched to me.

143

"Why didn't you go?"

"I have a little cold."

"What movie did they go to?"

"Ellie, why are you interrogating me?"

"Just tell me. You know how I am about little details."

"The new Harrison Ford thing, I don't remember the name."

Now, *that* I believed. Dad was the opposite of me when it came to details—unless those details were numbers.

"Will you tell her to call me when she gets home?"

"Of course."

Okay, I thought when I hung up the phone, my mom hated me so much for staying in this dangerous school that she had decided never to speak to me again. I lay on the sofa almost catatonic with despair. In her room, Candace had put on Melissa Etheridge, booming out "Come to My Window." Last year all Candace had ever played was Joan Armitrading albums. This year it was Etheridge. She was consistent in her tastes. She only liked strong women singers who sang passionate songs about— strong women.

Candace and I were getting along beautifully these days. As usual. But right now I felt so low I didn't even feel like talking to Candace. She was too happy. I was tired of being the miserable one.

So I called Abby instead.

"You sound horrible," I said, when she picked up.

"I'm not."

That was a switch. "Oh?"

"I'm so excited, as a matter of fact, that I'm about to faint."

I searched for the usual morose irony in her voice, didn't find it. "Tell me."

"Seth proposed to me tonight."

She still hadn't let down on the excited tone, but I knew she was faking. "I was right," I said. "You do sound horrible."

"Oh, come on. You can't even believe for one second that my life would work out?"

"Not all at once," I said, hedging.

"You sound horrible, too, by the way." She blew her nose.

"Are you crying?"

"Yes, but I'm blowing my nose because I have a wicked cold."

Abby was almost always sick. In the short time I had known her she'd had several colds, a bout of Asian flu, an ulcer, two horrible nosebleeds that wouldn't stop, and a hernia. She had spent more time at Barnard Health Services than anyone I knew. The day after I had given her the pepper pen, for instance, she had gone out to Amsterdam Avenue to try it out. She had held the pen several inches away from her—as per the pen's instructions—and sprayed it—

Right in her own eyes.

She'd spent the night in Columbia-Presbyterian hospital. When I visited her there, and she told me what had happened, I started laughing so hysterically that I could barely explain what had struck me funny. It was the image of Abby walking straight out of her dorm and spraying herself right in the eyes. I imagined someone—the guard at the dorm's security desk, say—watching her do that, how odd that must have looked, and I doubled over with giggles.

Her eyes hidden by bandages, Abby calmly told me that if I didn't stop laughing, she was going to kill herself—and then me. But I didn't—couldn't—stop and I actually think my laughing fit cheered her up a bit.

Now, when she stopped blowing her nose, she said, "I ran into Seth tonight."

"No! You have the worst luck. Where did you run into him?"

"Right outside his apartment building."

"Well, no wonder. What were you doing right outside his apartment building?"

"I was waiting for him to come out."

"Oh, Abby, you gotta give up on him already. He only makes you miserable."

"That's what he says."

"Well, he's right about that."

"But I can't be alone. I just can't."

There was a knock at our apartment door. I was pleased to see that my heart didn't immediately go into overdrive. I had gotten used to some of our Barnard neighbors stopping by to see Candace in the evening. Carmen and Jocelyn were in and out like they owned the place.

"Candace!" I called. "Someone at the door."

"Coming."

"Check the peephole."

"I will."

Candace padded by in a long Columbia T-shirt and slippers.

"Sorry," I told Abby. "But listen, about this alone business, that's really not true, because you already are alone."

"Oh, thanks a lot."

Down the long narrow hallway I could see Candace check the peephole, then undo the safety latch and swing the door open wide. The large head of old Molly came grinning into the apartment. I heard them talking and laughing.

"No, you know what I mean," I told Abby. "You're not with Seth and yet you're surviving."

"Barely."

"Not barely. And look at me. I'm not with anyone, and I'm surviving. And we're not alone. We've got friends, like each other."

Silence. I pictured Abby in her room, which was still utterly devoid of decoration. And then I remembered my promise to myself two months back, that I would buy her a poster. Tomorrow, I told myself.

Candace came back into the room with a tin of cookies that old Molly had brought by. I took one.

"I'm going down to talk to Molly," she told me.

Now that I had gotten to be friends with Molly, it made me a little jealous, all the other young friends Molly had—especially Candace. It was the same with Ruth. I wanted to be every mother's only child—or patient. But I nodded at Candace, blew a kiss, my mouth coated with cookie crumbs. "Thank you, Molly," I yelled out.

I heard her yell something back.

"What'd he say?" I asked Abby.

"Who?"

"Seth."

"He said he missed me."

"He did?"

"Uh-huh."

"Well, that's great. Then what are you feeling so down about?"

147

"The fact that I'm lying."

"Oh, he didn't say he missed you?"

"He said that if I kept bothering him, he would call the cops."

"He was joking, you know that."

"No," she sobbed, "he was serious."

"Abby, how often do you call him?"

"About twenty times a night."

"No, seriously . . ."

Silence.

"Abby, I don't like this new game where you lie all the time."

She snuffled.

"Abby?"

And then it hit me. She wasn't exaggerating.

"Abby! Twenty times a night?"

"I'm just . . . so obsessed with him. I let the phone ring and ring and ring. I want to fill up his apartment with rings so he can't even move and he has to call me back. Ellie, do you think maybe if I lost like twenty pounds he'd go out with me again?"

"Why? He needs to lose forty."

"I can't stop calling him. What's going to happen to me? I'm going to end up in jail."

"That's a laugh," I said. "Like the cops really care about someone getting a lot of phone calls from an ex-girlfriend when there's a serial killer on the loose. What does Ruth say?"

Abby didn't answer.

"Abby, what does Ruth say?"

"I don't know. I stopped going."

"You stopped going?!"

I had only been in therapy for a couple of months, but during that time I had changed from

148

being a total therapy-phobe to a fanatical therapy advocate. Everyone in the world should be in therapy, I was now convinced. I had even told old Molly to go. But certainly someone like Abby should never even consider—

"I already knew everything she was going to say," Abby said. "It got depressing. If I did something bad like call Seth lots of times, I didn't want to have the extra burden of knowing that Ruth would criticize me."

"She's not criticizing you, she's trying to help you understand yourself."

"To understand me is to criticize me," Abby said.

"That's not true," I said. But I laughed.

I looked at my watch. After eight. I'd eaten dinner at five. I was hungry again. "Hey, you want to go out and get some Mexican food?"

She sniffed. "It gives you a heart attack."

"So, what's one heart attack between friends?"

"I've got to go to the library."

"Now?"

"I've got a paper due tomorrow for sosh." (Which was what everyone called sociology.) "I haven't even started it. All-nighter city. Lots of fun when you have a cold."

"What's it on?"

"The Hemlock Society."

"You're joking. Abby, isn't that the group that helps people kill themselves?"

"Uh-huh."

"You're writing a paper about *that*?"

"I figured it was right up my alley."

"You're not *that* depressed, are you?"

She promised that she wasn't and that she would tell me if she was. I believed her. And after a few

149

more minutes of discussing the utter hopelessness of her life, I hung up, guiltily noticing that I was feeling ten times better than I had when I called her.

Instead of doing my reading for my theory-of-literature class, I watched *A Night at the Opera,* this old Marx brothers classic, on TV and ate an entire pint of Häagen-Daz rum-raisin and half a bag of caramelcorn. I had seen the movie maybe six times straight through and even more times in bits and pieces, but I was still whooping at the screen, it made me laugh so hard. I kept wishing Candace would come back upstairs so I could watch it with her.

After the movie was over, I wondered if Candace was all right, she'd been gone so long. But before I could get too scared about that, on came another old classic, *Double Indemnity,* with my favorite movie star of all time, the woman I wanted to be in my next life if I couldn't be Candace—Barbara Stanwyck. I was halfway through that movie when Candace came back upstairs.

"You'll never believe what happened," she said.

"Candace, quiet, this is the part where Edward G. Robinson starts to catch on that there's been a double cross and Barbara Stanwyck has to hide behind the door."

"I'm down there, talking to old Molly, right? There's a knock at the door."

"Candace, shush."

"It's this old guy with a big bushy beard."

That got my attention. "What did he look like?"

"I just told you."

"No, but I mean, more specifically."

I was picturing the man that Molly had pointed out to me that day in the garden.

"Tall, bony, big beard," Candace said. "Why don't you ever let me tell you a story without interrupting?"

"Long silver hair, all slicked back?"

"Yeah, how did you know? So anyway, Molly goes *berserk*. Gets her broom. Starts shouting at him to go away. Beating on the door with the broom. I loved it. That woman is a wildcat. I hope I'll be that feisty when I'm her age."

"You'll be twice as feisty when you're three times her age."

"No way."

"So then what happened?"

"The guy's drunk, crying, begging to be let in. Finally she opens the door and smacks him with the broom. The wooden end. Bam! Right on the top of his head. Right on the old noggin."

"No! Was he okay?"

"Oh, yeah. She didn't hit *that* hard. But it sobered him up, let me tell you. She's yelling at him about not coming around drunk like a skunk. And he starts shambling away and saying he misses her. Turns out, this is Molly's boyfriend or something. Who knew?"

"Yeah," I said. "*I* knew. That's Fred. He's a drunk."

I was trying to show off that I knew more about Molly than she did. But Candace just smiled approvingly. "You know everything. Anyway, he was sure drunk tonight. Some idiot let him into the building."

I went back to watching the TV.

"That's it?" Candace said. "I tell you a great story like that and you can't stop watching your stupid movie? Does the term *couch potato* mean anything to you?"

151

"Shut up and watch," I said. "This is one of the best movies ever made."

Candace sighed. "You're hopeless."

"Just sit down."

"That woman has some amazing stories," she said. She sat down next to me on the sofa and reached her hand noisily into the foil bag of popcorn. "She was telling me her whole life, before that old wino showed up and sent her off the deep end. Did you know old Molly once saved a Barnard girl who had jumped into the Hudson?"

I had heard that story about the drowning girl, for one, and also I wished that Molly would only share her stories with me. "Candace," I said, "please, just watch for one minute. If you're not hooked after a minute, I won't bother you anymore."

She didn't watch. I did, listening with only half an ear to Candace repeating Molly's stories. About half an hour later both Candace and I got tired of what we were doing and went to bed.

It was after midnight.

Later, I would be pretty sure of the schedule of all these events, because I could match them up with the movies on TV.

The next day after my last class (Chinese history, which had proved to be even more boring than I had feared) I shopped for a poster for Abby's room. I picked out one of Marlon Brando in *A Streetcar Named Desire,* which I have always personally thought is the sexiest performance in all movie history. When he's at the bottom of the stairs in that ripped sweaty T-shirt screaming out for his wife, "STELLAAAAA!" I get all woozy. I have a copy of that movie. When he's shouting for Stella, I try to hear "Ellie!" in my head instead. The names are pretty close. What can I tell you? It's a thrill.

I walked up to Plimpton, twirling the poster tube like a baton.

"Stelllaaaa!" I yelled in my best Brando voice as I walked down the gloomy hallway to Abby's room. "Come down here, Stella!"

I found Abby's door wide-open.

A cop was inside, talking with one of Abby's neighbors.

The girl looked scared.

Both the cop and the girl turned to look at me.

"Where's Abby?" I asked.

The girl's answer whammed all my new confidence right out of me. It felt like when you get the wind knocked out of you and you can't breathe.

"We don't know," the girl said. "No one's seen her since last night."

CHAPTER 21

MY VERY FIRST THOUGHT WAS THAT ABBY
had killed herself.

In fact, I was heart-sinkingly sure this was true. The
cop took down everything I could remember about
Abby's mood the night before, and each fact I
described sounded like another reason for Abby to do
herself in. The way the cop kept glancing at me, I
began to squirm. I wondered if he was thinking what I
was thinking. How could I have just hung up on Abby
last night? How could I have let her go?

I had to repeat the whole story for the homicide
detectives, including Detective Pearl, and for a group
of FBI agents led by Agent Wilkins. There were no
smiles in the room the whole time I was talking.

As late as Wednesday night we were still hoping that
Abby had run away. But by Thursday, two days after
Abby had disappeared, the police had ruled out a run-
away or suicide and with tense chagrined faces were
admitting to reporters that Abby's case looked suspi-
ciously like attack number four of the Barnard killer.

Natural-born leaders, like Candace, need a major

crisis before their skills can really come into play. Abby's disappearance had given Candace her greatest challenge; it was no surprise to me that she rose to the task at once. That night she had her Find Jenny (it was now Find Jenny and Abby) members marching around the streets with megaphones calling for a midnight rally on campus. She had borrowed a mike from the theater department. And at midnight she gave a passionate speech about how we all had to band together now, all of us Barnard girls.

She had some practical suggestions about a buddy system—only going outside in the evenings in pairs. But most of the speech was fiery and emotional.

"Abby Rovere is missing," she cried. "Jenny Silver is missing. But we're here. You and you and you. We're here. And we have to ask ourselves, Barnard. We have to ask ourselves, how much are we going to let this killer get away with? How many victims will we let this killer strike down? Now, I know a lot of you are thinking about going home. Hey, I'm thinking about it, too. But you know what? *This* is my home."

There were cheers.

"Right here. Look around you. This is my home. Are we going to let this killer destroy our school, our education, our lives? Or are we going to use these horrible tragedies to band together and fight back?"

A bigger cheer.

I was watching from the back of the crowd. I couldn't listen anymore. I just started walking, out the gates, down Broadway, following the same route that Jenny must have followed on her last night on earth. Though I was bundled into my overcoat and had the hood up, I was freezing—and not from the cold weather. The cold was inside me.

155

I sat in our usual booth at Tom's Diner and was ruder to Arlene than Arlene usually was to us. I ordered a cup of coffee and just sat with it in silence.

I had a decision to make, and it horrified me.

It was a decision that had already seemed to make itself.

I knew what I had to do.

I guess I was hoping I could talk myself out of it.

CHAPTER 22

ON FRIDAY NIGHT I WENT BACK TO THE police station and told them a few more meaningless details that had occurred to me about Abby. When I got back home, the apartment was jammed with twice the usual number that attended the Find Jenny committee meetings. The phone started ringing as I walked in the door.

As Candace moved to answer the phone she sawed the air with her hand, saying, "I think a march on the police station would make a statement to the media that—"

She grabbed the receiver and barked a hello. "Just a sec." She held the phone out to me. I took it. Everyone in the room was staring at me with the somber respect that went with being Abby's best friend. I was truly part of the inner circle now. I was the closest living survivor of victim number 4.

Candace went on with her reasons for staging a placard-carrying protest about police inaction on the case. As soon as I found out the call was from my mother—she was shrieking—I took the phone in my bedroom and shut the door.

"Mom," I said. "Mom—Mom—you're not letting me finish what I'm— *Mom!* Listen to me. Not every girl at Barnard is going home for the semester, that's just not true. *Which* news broadcast? Well, I'm right here, Mom, I'm right in the middle of it, and I can tell you—"

I couldn't tell her a thing. She was back to shrieking again.

The truth was, the Barnard campus was beginning to look like the footage you saw on the news of those tiny foreign countries right before the collapse of their democratic governments. Despite Candace's pleas, there were girls with suitcases everywhere you looked, hugging each other good-bye, or out in the street shouting for taxis, or climbing into the back of their parents' cars. There was only a month left to Christmas break, and a lot of girls weren't sticking around.

On the other hand, it was amazing that *anyone* was sticking around. Probably the whole campus would have gone if it hadn't been for Candace.

"Mom . . . the fact of the matter is, most of the—most of the students are staying. No, they are not insane. Look, this is New York City. I mean, what's one more serial killer more or less?"

After that crack, I had to hold the receiver away from my ear, because my mother was making so much noise. I sighed deeply, trying to catch my breath. I could never make my mother understand—never. Truth was, I didn't fully understand it myself.

Since the day that Abby had vanished, I had been feeling almost constant terror. Sometimes I got so scared it was hard for me to talk. But I owed it to

Abby to stay, it was that simple. I had to find out what had happened to my friend.

Outside my window, through the bars of the metal gate, I could see the neon red flashing letters, AR, from the bar sign. Only now the sign seemed like part of my conscience, flashing Abby's initials on, off, on, off.

Killer or no killer . . . I was going to stick this thing out.

All the way to the bloody end.

CHAPTER 23

I SAT IN ON THE REST OF CANDACE'S MEETING. Candace gave me a surprised but grateful look. I nodded back.

When everyone had left I said, "I want to go over everything we know about Abby's last night. I want to take it step-by-step, just like we did with Jenny. Maybe we can find her. And stop looking at me like that."

"I'm just proud of you, that's all."

"Well, don't be, because this is all a façade and it could crumble at any second." I had bought a brand-new Barnard loose-leaf notebook. I turned to the first page. My hand was trembling.

"So," I said, writing as I talked, "we know she went to the library."

"How do we know?" Candace asked.

"Because she said she was going to the library."

"So? Maybe she changed her mind."

I tossed the pen down in disgust. "So then we know nothing."

"Okay," Candace said, "let's say she started

160

toward the library. We can figure that much, because her sosh paper was due the next day."

I looked at my watch. I stood. "Okay," I said. "Let's get going. We'll go from Plimpton to the library and see if we can find anything."

Walking down icy Amsterdam Avenue at night in the dead of winter had never seemed so scary to me, even with Candace trudging next to me. We walked all the way down the hill to Plimpton, then back up to the Columbia campus and through the giant gates.

The main quad at Columbia is huge and vast. It's even got a tennis court next to some of the admin buildings. The library is gigantic, a white marble building with a long flight of marble steps, a floating iceberg gleaming in the winter moonlight.

We showed our ID cards to the security guard at the door, then showed him one of the flyers Candace had printed up with a snapshot of Abby I'd found in my room. The guard said, "Like I told the cops, there are so many students in here every night, I couldn't possibly remember whether—"

"I'm going to go check the stacks," I told Candace, "you see what you can find out from book checkout."

"Right."

I looked in the card catalog under *Hemlock Society* and *Suicide* and jotted down a few main call numbers. Mostly the suicide books seemed to be in the 614s and the 179s. Then I showed my ID card to another guard and went up into the vast library stacks.

The stacks of the Columbia library are dark quiet halls filled with the odor of dusty old books. It smelled like pure knowledge in there, like if you breathed deeply for long enough, you could inhale yourself into a genius. There was no sound except for the occasional hum as someone turned on one of the timer lights at the end of each row of shelves. I found the call numbers for Abby's cheerful sociology topic and turned the timer light all the way to the right. The fluorescents fluttered to life. The timer began to hum and wheeze like a bomb ticking down to a massive explosion.

Mixed in with a lot of books on medicine, I found several books on suicide. I didn't like the titles. They gave me the creeps.

Rita Marker, *Deadly Compassion*, 614.31.

Christian Barnard, *Good Life, Good Death*, 616.858.

I started leafing through a book on the psychology of suicide. If Abby had come to the library, wouldn't she have taken these books out?

"In psychological terms, then," I read, "we can say that the suicide is the most destructive act known to man. In its utter violation of the ego and all of one's own natural instincts for survival, the suicide represents the worst form of mental illness. To kill another is at least an expression of one's anger, a way of getting the anger *out*. To kill oneself is to turn the anger inward on its self to ensure that the anger will never be truly expressed."

Great, I thought, putting the book back on its shelf. So this psychiatrist was claiming that the serial killer out there was mentally healthier than someone like Abby, who was always so depressed. That was really—

I stopped breathing. I had heard footsteps. My hand started to shake so badly that I didn't get the book back on the shelf, and when it hit the floor it

162

sounded like a gunshot. I nearly fainted. I bent down, picked up the book, slid it back onto the shelf, probably in the wrong spot, but I sure didn't care. I listened some more.

Silence.

Except for the droning hum of the hall light, I heard nothing. The timer clicked a few times. The hum was getting higher in pitch now. . . .

That meant I was running out of time.

I wanted to run.

I told myself, firmly, *no*.

I stared down at the slip of paper in my hand where I had scribbled the call numbers. There was one number I had underlined. 617.82. That was the call number for the book specifically about the Hemlock Society. If there was one book Abby was likely to take out, that was it. I realized something. If she checked for that book first and found it was in, she might have decided she didn't need any others. She was going to be pulling an all-nighter, after all; how many books could she use and read in one night?

I started tracing my finger along the spines of the books.

614.89 . . .

615.25 . . .

When I found the 616s I had reached the end of the aisle. I turned around. The numbers were going up. So I was still in the right row. My finger still on the spines of the books in front of me, I started coming back the other way.

616.74 . . .

617.11 . . .

Here we go.

And then, I found it.

617.81 . . .

And 617.83.

Right where the book should have been, there was a gap.

Maybe Abby had taken the book out after all!

And that meant she *had* been in the library . . . and we could trace at least part of her route. I stepped closer to the shelf, peering at the book spines, wanting to make doubly sure the book wasn't here.

I opened my mouth.

No sound came out.

There was a face in the gap on the shelf, a pair of eyes studying me.

And then the light in the aisle clicked off, plunging me into darkness.

CHAPTER 24

I LET OUT A BLOODCURDLING SCREAM. AT least it curdled *my* blood. I fell back against the shelf behind me, scattering books. And then I started to run.

But I could hear the killer running down the next aisle along with me, and when I came out the end of the aisle into the dim light of the hallway, there he was.

Stuart Englander.

"I'm sorry," he was saying over and over. "I didn't mean to scare you."

Pounding footsteps now as students ran toward us from all directions. A scream in the library late at night would have been enough to bring a crowd at any time, but with everything that had been going on lately, my scream really got a dramatic response.

"I was . . . looking for books for my writing project . . ." he said, "and then, suddenly, I saw you through the stacks. I was pretty scared . . . too."

Someone shoved their way through the crowd. Candace. I told her, when I could breathe again, what had happened. People were already drifting away, heading back to their carrels and their studying.

"Hey, Candace," Stuart said, his face lighting up.

After our disastrous double date that night, Stuart had had the nerve to pursue Candace for a few days more. But she had been extremely firm and convinced him his chances were somewhat less than zero. He gave up, and I hadn't seen him since.

Candace grabbed my shaking hand and squeezed. "It's okay," she told me. Which helped a lot. It helped convince my body that everything was indeed okay. I was still in fight-or-flight mode.

To Stuart, Candace said, "Seems like a pretty big coincidence, you being here, now, doesn't it?"

"Sure does," he agreed.

"Where were you Tuesday night, the night Abby disappeared? Right here, lurking in the stacks?"

Stuart blinked. "What is this?"

"It's a question," Candace said. "Answer it."

"Tuesday night . . . no, I wasn't in the library Tuesday night. Some guys from the swim team—we went to the Rangers game at the Garden Tuesday night. *Why?*"

"Like who . . . on the team?" I asked.

He rattled off several names with utter confidence.

"C'mon," Candace said, taking my arm, leading me away.

"You accusing me of something?" Stuart called after us.

"We'll see," Candace shot back.

When we were downstairs, I told her what I'd found out.

"I found out the same thing," Candace said. "She checked the book out."

166

"The police must have found that much out, too" I said.

"I doubt it."

We went outside the library, stood on the freezing steps. Candace used the little campus phone outside the library and called campus information. She got the room number for one of the swim jocks that Stuart had named as his Tuesday-night alibi. The guy said yeah, he and Stu had been at the Rangers game.

"Dead end," Candace said as she hung up.

"Not yet," I said. "Let's think. We're standing right where Abby stood that night. She's got the book. What would Abby do next?"

"Play a game of late-night tennis," Candace suggested, staring across at the fenced-in court.

"Or she might have come by to see me," I said. "I asked her if she wanted to get some Mex food."

Then I had another idea. I picked up the campus phone and dialed.

"Security."

"Hi, this is Ellie Sommers, a Barnard student. I'm at the main campus. I need to go to Plimpton."

"Okay," the guard said, "wait by the main gate on Amsterdam, the van will swing by to get you in . . . about twenty minutes."

"Twenty minutes!" I said, raising my eyebrows at Candace.

"We're crazy busy right now," the guard said apologetically. "We've never had so many calls before. Everyone's pretty scared, you know."

I could believe that.

"What about last Tuesday night? You have any record of an Abby Rovere calling for the van around this time of night?"

167

"Oh, geez, we don't keep any records like that."

"Were you on duty Tuesday night?"

"Yeah, I was."

"Do you remember an Abby Rovere calling—"

"Hold on," he said, and went away for a moment. When he came back on, he said, "Listen, I've got about a hundred calls coming in here, so if—"

"Do you remember a call from an Abby Rovere on Tuesday night?" I asked, raising my voice.

I saw the look Candace was giving me. Raising my voice, insisting on anything—it wasn't part of my usual repertoire. I could see she was pleased.

"To be honest with you, I have absolutely no idea," the guard said.

Raising my voice hadn't been very effective, but it still felt good. "Thanks," I said as curtly as I could.

"Just wait by the gate and the van will be by."

"No," I said. "Forget the van."

"Hey," the guard said. "Do me a favor. Wait for the van. Don't go walking."

The words went through me like ice.

"I won't," I promised, "I'll take a taxi."

I hung up.

"What's wrong?" Candace asked.

"He told me not to walk."

"So?"

We stared at each other as the idea crystallized in both our brains at the same time.

I could see my own amazement and terror reflected in Candace's face.

When we spoke we spoke in unison.

"She walked," we both said.

CHAPTER 25

"WE'RE BOTH GENIUSES," CANDACE SAID AFTER she took her hand off her mouth and stopped gasping.

"We don't know for sure."

"Of course we do. I do anyway. The van was busy and she got impatient and she was depressed anyway, so she figured what the hell, I hope I get killed. And she walked. She walked she walked she walked."

"To Plimpton by herself late at night?"

"Yes!"

I was determined to shoot down my own theory. I was so excited—I couldn't believe we had figured this out—that I was sure some major flaw in our argument was going to swoop down on us any second.

"If she was impatient for the security van, she still could have walked over to see me," I said, "or gone and hung out at Seth's building and tried to get in to see him. She was completely obsessed with the guy. God knows why. What if—"

"No."

"Candace, don't say no to me like that ever again. I'm serious. I've told you before."

169

"No no no no."

"All right," I said, crossing my arms, "if it's no, tell me why. Try to be logical for once in your life."

Candace smiled confidently. "She had a paper to write. She had a cold. She was going to be up all night. She didn't have time for Seth, no matter how obsessed she was. And she certainly didn't have time for you."

My heart was thumping. I nodded. "She walked," I said.

We started walking, icy air pluming out of our mouths.

"You really are brilliant, you know that?" Candace told me.

"Yeah, I know," I said.

My voice shook. Candace must have noticed, because she said, "You sure you want to do this?"

"Don't ask me that."

We went out through the gates onto Amsterdam and turned left. Our second trip to Plimpton in one night. We were walking uptown, but the street plummeted down, down the big hill.

"Ellie?"

"What?"

"Don't look now, but I think that car is following us. I *said* don't look now."

It was a black car cruising slowly in the darkness, like a shark swimming after its prey. I couldn't see who was inside.

We quickened our pace.

I wasn't the only one who was looking back. So was Candace.

So neither one of us saw the man step out of the shadows in *front* of us until—

It was too late.

CHAPTER 26

"SPARE SOME CHANGE?" THE MAN ASKED, shoving a hand at us.

We both jumped, then swung out wide into the street to get away from him. That was one of those safety rules they taught you in Manhattan. When you were in trouble, get right out into the street where the cars could see you.

Except right now I didn't see any cars. Even that black car that had been cruising us would have been a welcome sight. But no . . .

The panhandler was a tall young man with a grimy greenish face. He was wearing one of those knitted ski caps that I had come to associate with horrible crimes. He started after us, walking with a slight limp. "C'mon," he said, "help me out a little here. I'm freezing my ass off. Can't you help me with a little change to get a cup of coffee?"

I grabbed Candace at the same time Candace grabbed me. We were both clutching each other with icy frostbitten hands. We started to run.

I don't know which one of us had the idea to turn right. It was more like we were playing with the Ouija board, and our movements were the result of both of our instincts rather than any rational thought.

Whoever's instincts they were, they were terrible.

Turning right meant turning down the next deserted cross-street.

The panhandler ran limping after us.

And now we were on a narrow cross street.

There was even less chance of a car coming by and saving us.

We ran faster. Crossed another intersection, kept going.

Then we stopped.

We were on a very bad block.

Manhattan is like that, the good parts and the bad parts are right next to each other. The city changes magically and demonically almost block by block.

On either side of us rose a wall of burned-out buildings with plywood covering some of the windows and nasty graffiti spray-painted everywhere. Broken glass glittered in the street like diamonds. It was the kind of street I had seen on the news hundreds of times as they reported drug busts and stray shootings and other urban violence. Before now I had only set foot on a street like this in my nightmares.

And then the panhandler turned the corner behind us. He began limping slowly and steadily after us. There was no place to go but farther down this street, farther into urban hell.

We started running again. The icy wind cut my lungs like a razor. I clawed at my hood, trying to push it off my head, because I had zipped it up tight and the rim of white fur that fringed the hood was blocking my vision. When I got the hood off, I saw them.

Three tough-looking teenagers standing in a loose knot outside a run-down building across the street. One of them was carrying a long wooden stick, like you used in stickball, except I didn't think that's what these kids were using it for. I saw a bus kiosk about half a block away from them, its glass walls shattered into tiny bits that were still hanging in the metal frame.

The teenagers were staring right at me and Candace, and the look in their eyes went right through me. We were prey.

We couldn't go back because the panhandler was coming that way. So we tried to run faster.

I was praying we would make it to the next block, where I could see a store or two. But the kids moved fast. In a flash, they were across the street.

"Hey, girls, whatcha doin'?"

We skidded to a halt, ready to run back the other way, panhandler or no panhandler. But another kid had magically appeared behind us, and he had something in his hand.

And then there was a click as the object in the kid's hand flicked open and gleamed in the streetlights.

It was a switchblade.

By now Candace was screaming, and maybe I was, too, I don't even know. As—

The muggers moved in on us from all sides.

CHAPTER 27

I FINALLY REALIZED WHAT CANDACE WAS screaming. Not just *"Help!"* She was screaming at me to use my pepper spray. She was using hers. Spraying it right and left. And I saw several of our attackers clutch their eyes in pain.

One of the kids had a hold of me, and I was screaming and trying to pull myself free. And then Candace got the pen right in his face and *Psssst!*—the kid fell. While he was down Candace kicked him in the groin for good measure.

But there were more kids now, and one of them knocked the pen out of Candace's hand.

And now Candace was screaming again, and this time she was screaming at me to run. I saw her running down the street. I told my legs to move.

They didn't.

I was as frozen and paralyzed with fear as I had been in my nightmares night after night. And then someone grabbed me. I struggled to free myself. Got free. More hands. Yanking my hair. Slapping me. Knocking me down.

I hit the sidewalk hard, felt the ground smack my head. I tried to get to my feet. Just as—

Candace came running back and tackled my attacker. They went down together in a heap. But the kid was tall and strong and he rolled over, pinning Candace underneath him. He started banging her head down against the sidewalk over and over.

I threw myself at him, but I felt as if my entire body had been smacked hard with a rubber hammer and all my limbs were asleep and useless. I slapped at the teenager helplessly, meaninglessly. He didn't even seem to feel the blows.

And then I saw the kid with the stick.

He had raised it high in the air, right over my head.

CHAPTER 28

BUT BEFORE HE COULD SWING AT ME, SOME-
one swung at him. I heard the thud of metal hitting
skull, and the boy dropped straight to his knees, so
that briefly we were face-to-face. And then he sank
against me, sliding down fast, hitting the sidewalk.

The man who had hit him struck again, this time
clobbering the boy who had hold of Candace.

At the same time there were sirens, and cars
were converging on us from all sides. They weren't
cop cars, just normal-looking cars. One car was
black and vaguely familiar looking, with a movable
siren placed on top, spinning its bright blue-and-red
lights in my face. Doors were flying open, people
were running.

And then I saw who had saved us. It was the panhandler with the limp. He didn't seem to be limping
now as he rushed around the sidewalk, putting hand-
cuffs on several of our attackers.

I was crying. Soundlessly. Fluid just seemed to be
gushing out of my eyes and nose. I was holding on to

Candace and she was holding on to me. I was rocking her.

And then somebody swore, and when I looked up I saw the familiar face of Agent Wilkins.

Agent Wilkins personally accompanied us to the hospital ER to make sure we were okay. Which we were, except for some bad scratches, bumps, and bruises. Since Candace hadn't blacked out, they were pretty sure she hadn't received a concussion. We were supposed to call right away if she started vomiting, ran a fever, felt lethargic, or experienced what the intern called "a change in mental status."

"I've been experiencing that all semester," I said.

The doctor didn't laugh. "Also," he said, "of course, if you lose consciousness."

"If I lose consciousness I promise I'll call you," Candace told him.

Agent Wilkins drove us home in that same black car we had seen cruising behind us on Amsterdam. The panhandler, it turned out, was one of Wilkins's own men. It seemed that the FBI and the cops had done the same research we had done about Abby's route on Tuesday night. They'd been staking out the area ever since.

On the other hand, Agent Wilkins doubted that anything bad could have happened to Abby if she had walked back to Plimpton that night—because the whole campus area was already crawling with cops and agents.

"Something bad happened to us," Candace pointed out from the backseat.

Agent Wilkins had looked furious the whole time we were dealing with the doctors and the nurses. He looked even madder now. "If you're blaming us for what happened to you tonight"—his jaw clenched—"then I think I might be about to lose my temper."

Wilkins had been so polite in all my dealings with him; I didn't want to see him get angry—ever.

We sat in silence for a few moments. I stared out the window at our boot of a building. Home. A few lights were on. Molly wasn't out front.

"I just don't know what it is with you two," Agent Wilkins said finally.

Here it comes, I thought. He's going to blow his stack.

"You have a death wish or what?"

"We're just trying to find out what happened to our friends," I said. I was crying again, as I had on and off since the attack. I didn't even know when the tears were coming, I'd just feel the wetness running down my cheeks.

Angrily, Agent Wilkins reached over and popped open the glove compartment. There was a flashlight buckled up under the lid, and on top of the super-neat pile of maps and registration forms was a packet of Kleenex. He handed them to me.

"This is my fault," Candace said. "I've been goading her into doing something, you know, to find Jenny—for months—and—"

"It's not your fault," I told her. I blew my nose definitively, as if that ended the argument.

"I don't really care whose fault it is," Agent Wilkins said dryly. "Let me try to explain this to you one last time, because at the rate you two are

178

going, I may not get another chance. Every crime ever committed, from first-degree murder right down to petty theft, is a crime of opportunity. You understand what I'm telling you? What if you walked into a store and there was no one inside the store at that moment and the register was wide-open and there were hundreds of dollars, just lying there, staring back at you, begging to be taken? Anyone would be tempted to reach into that till, right?

"Well, if the two of you keep walking around Manhattan begging to be killed, there are plenty of people who are going to crawl out of the woodwork and do the job."

I handed the Kleenex packet back to him and mumbled, "Thanks." He reached back across me, put the Kleenex back in position on top of the maps, snapped the glove compartment door shut with a bang. His walkie-talkie rasped to life. He talked for a few minutes, explaining to some other agents that he was dropping us off. He gave our address.

"Okay," he said finally, "that's all. You can go now."

I didn't move. All my mentor love had washed back over me full-force. After everything that had happened, right then, at that moment, I wanted nothing in life so badly as for Agent Wilkins to forgive me and not be mad at me any longer and hug me and protect me. But instead all he did was reach across me one last time and open the front door for me. It wasn't a friendly gesture. It said, "Get out."

"You two have been very lucky," he said as we

179

piled out of the car. "You want to take any bets on how long that luck is going to last?"

I was still crying as we filed into the building. I glanced back and waved, as if Agent Wilkins were our dear close friend. He waited until we were safely inside, then drove away.

I wonder what it cost to have your own special FBI agent as a bodyguard? Could we hire Agent Wilkins to stop searching for the serial killer and just live in the lobby and protect us?

Back in the apartment we silently took all the food that looked half-decent out of the fridge and sat around the living room stuffing it in our faces with the ravenous hunger of those who have recently escaped death.

When we were finally sated, and had stopped belching loudly, Candace said, "I'm sorry."

"Why?"

"That was like your worst nightmare, wasn't it?"

"Yeah. Literally. But it wasn't your fault. It was my idea, remember? And it was a good one. Sort of."

That weekend I went home. Not for good, I promised Candace; just to visit. But that wasn't what I had in mind and I think Candace knew it, though she didn't say anything. I felt guilty leaving her alone in the apartment at a time like this. But it was like . . . ever since Abby had vanished, my confidence and my bravery kept flickering like a candle flame about to go out. I was praying that my mother would kidnap me and tie me to the bed in my room and never let me return to the war zone that was college.

Home. As unhappy a place as it had been for me, the house in Englewood still meant safety to me.

I had to go.

My mother gave me a long hard hug at the door. So long a hug that I started to feel uncomfortable. She was crying. I could feel her tears on my cheek.

"Okay, okay," Dad was saying, "Marcia, c'mon, let's let her get inside. It's cold out there. C'mon, dear, let's get the door closed at least. Marcia—"

We sat in the kitchen, which had always been the main meeting room in our house. I chattered on and on, trying to present a ridiculously cheerful portrait of my life at school, leaving gaping holes where all the stuff that really was happening should have gone. My father was trying to be cheerful, too, but I had never seen him look so ashen and worn-out and worried.

My mother didn't say much, just kept giving me this blank level stare that I didn't like one bit. Periodically through my childhood she'd had these semi-breakdowns where she'd just take to her room and her bed and not come out for weeks at a time. I wondered if she'd had another one of those episodes and no one was telling me.

Finally Dad went into the den to watch *Mystery Theater* on PBS and we were alone.

"So how have you been?" I asked Mom. I had my mouth crammed full with Mallomars so my question came out only semi-audibly.

Mom shrugged. "Good," she said like a zombie.

"Are you still taking the Prozac?"

"Mm-hmm."

"Is it helping?"

Another shrug.

"Mom," I said, "I know I've become like a broken record about this, but I can't believe you'd be willing to take medication but you're not willing to go to therapy. Ruth has really helped me."

"Oh, I'm sure," my mother said, looking pained.

"She has."

"Oh, I know, I know."

"What's that supposed to mean?"

"Well—I mean—everything out of your mouth these days is Ruth, Ruth, Ruth, Ruth, Ruth."

Too late—yet again—I realized my mistake.

"You're jealous of her, aren't you?"

Mom rolled her eyes.

"Mom, she's my therapist. She's not my mother. That's a very different thing. There is no competition here. I mean, I already have a mother. A wonderful mother."

I reached for my mother's hand, she pulled it away.

"I'm sure," said Mom, "that I made a lot of mistakes. But you wait till you have children. You'll see, it's not so easy."

"Who said you made mistakes?"

"Oh, I'm sure that's what you and this Ruth do all day, just sit around laughing about how horrible and crazy I am."

"No!"

I could hear the sounds of Dad's TV show floating in from the den: British voices, laughter, gunshots.

"Mom," I said, "it's not like that. If you would try therapy, you would see." I repeated Candace's line. "Just try one session."

"I can't."

"Why?"

"Oh, for goodness' sakes, Ellie. Englewood is a small town. It's like a fishbowl. If I went to therapy, everyone would know. They'd all start talking about me."

"No, they wouldn't."

We batted this back and forth for a few minutes and then my mother leaned forward and lowered her voice. "Ellie."

"What?"

"They already hate me."

She was whispering.

"Who hates you?" I asked.

"Not so loud. The whole town. They're banding together. They despise me. They hold meetings."

"What meetings? What are you talking about?"

"Secret meetings. Where they talk about their little plots against me. They've all agreed not to be as friendly as they used to, like in the grocery store. They give me funny looks."

I suddenly felt so light-headed, I was surprised I didn't float around the room. "They give you funny looks," I said, "because you never like to talk to anyone and you go out so rarely."

"That's just it. That's why I don't go out much. Because it's not safe. They are all in it together, I'm telling you. Your father knows all about it, but he does nothing to stop it. Well, what can he do? He's not a strong man. . . ."

She went on and on, first in a whisper, then back to her normal voice. If you could use that word in this context.

Because what she was saying was not normal.

Not normal at all.

* * *

"She said *that*?"

"Yes."

"Well then, she was joking."

"Candace, she was not joking. She was dead serious."

I was in my room, sitting on the bed, making wild gestures with my free hand to emphasize my points, though Candace of course could not see me. It was two in the morning. I had woken up Candace for once. I was crying, as usual.

"What does your dad say?"

"I couldn't get him alone to talk about it, but I saw the look on his face when he came into the kitchen. First he had this big phony smile. But then there was this terror in his eyes when he saw the look on my face. And he starts asking, 'What have you two been chattering about?' Of course he knows. Oh, God, Candace, this is my mother—"

"Well, look, Ellie, they have medication for this kind of thing. It's not the end of the world. It's a chemical imbalance. I mean, there's no stigma attached. It's just a problem. A medical problem. Is she on anything besides the Prozac? Maybe something she's taking is giving her a paranoid reaction."

"No. She's not taking anything else."

I had the sudden terrifying thought that my mother might be listening at the door or on another extension. Now who was the paranoid one? I got so frightened I had to put the phone down and go check. A dark empty hallway. And no sounds coming from the closed door to my parents' bedroom.

When I got back to my room, though, I had a terrifying flash of insight. My mouth fell open wide. Someone could have stuck their fist in my mouth right then and it wouldn't have touched my lips. I started shaking violently.

"Candace," I said when I picked up the receiver. "I just had a very scary thought."

"What?"

"I . . . can't say."

"Why not?"

"Too scary."

"Okay," Candace said, "even though I haven't heard it yet, I can already promise you that what you are about to say is just going to be your overactive imagination at work once again. How's that?"

"Remember how I told you that my mother took those classes at Columbia, the general-education courses?"

"No, but go ahead."

"Six years ago she took one, and two."

"So?"

"Six years ago. Two years ago. Leiter. Sanchez."

"Oh my God. Are you sure, about the dates, I mean?"

"Positive."

"Okay," Candace said, "but wait—wait—wait! You're forgetting it again, Ellie. Motive. Your mother has the least motive of anyone I know."

"She's always been really jealous of my father's young students," I said in a monotone. "Obsessively, crazily jealous."

"No," Candace said, but not the way she usually said it, more like she was pleading with me to stop.

"Why not?" I asked. "Go ahead, show me what's wrong with my theory. Please."

"It's circumstantial, that's what's wrong with it.

185

You're just really upset because you just found out your mother is a psycho, pardon the expression, but Ellie, there are all kinds of mental illness in this world, and only a few kinds are murderers, okay? Ellie?"

I didn't answer.

Because while Candace was talking I had looked up.

My mom was standing in the dark shadows of my bedroom, staring at me.

CHAPTER 29

"TALKING BAD AGAINST YOUR OWN MOTHER,"
she said quietly.

"I gotta go," I said to Candace.

I could hear Candace's tiny voice yelling at me to
hold on as I placed the receiver back in its cradle.

"Mom," I said. "What are you—"

She stepped toward me, taking the odd purposeful
giant steps I had seen used by homeless women on
the street. She got right in my face, too, putting her
own face an inch from mine. She was shouting now,
*"You talk against your own mother! You're part of
the conspiracy! Aren't you? My only child! My only
daughter! Conspiring against me!"*

It went on. Seconds, a minute, I don't know,
except that it was the lowest moment of my life.
Sometime during this spewing of bile and rage Dad
charged into the room in his bathrobe, silver hair
wildly mussed with sleep. And then he had Mom by
the shoulders and he was begging her to come back
to the bedroom. "Not in front of Ellie," he kept saying
to her. "Not in front of Ellie."

187

I heard yelling from the bedroom for about twenty minutes more. I sat on the cedar chest in the hallway, waiting. Once when I was six I accidentally broke my mother's favorite china platter. Mom had made me wait here in this exact spot while she cried in her bedroom. It had been the most interminable wait of my life—until now.

There was silence from their bedroom. I swung my bare legs back and forth like a little girl. I thought about what Candace had said about my theory. She was right. Just a coincidence, I told myself. And then I tried to shut the door firmly on that idea. I was so horrified by what I had just seen—my mother raving like that—that I had no room in my heart to think of her as serial killer as well.

Finally the bedroom door opened and my father came out.

"Your mother wants to talk to you," he said.

I went in. Mom was sitting up in bed, looking at me with dark hollow eyes. She looked like a little girl. "I just want to say . . . that I'm very sorry I lost my temper like that. And I hope—"

She started crying. So did I.

"I hope you won't go back to school just because I behaved so badly. I hope that you will live with us forever—and e-ever." She was sobbing now.

My father hurried to her. He was holding her. I stayed for a few minutes, standing helplessly and miserably at the foot of the bed, then went back outside.

Dad found me in my bedroom. I was packing.

"Where are you going?"

"Back to school."

"It's the middle of the night."

"I've got to leave."

"Ellie, it's not safe, it's no time for you to be out, and with everything that's been happening in New York, I mean, my God, it's—"

I turned on him. "You lied to me."

He looked frightened. "Ellie, I—"

"Don't deny it. You lied to me. I've been asking you how Mom is for months. And every time you told me she was just feeling a little worried—you lied, you lied, you lied."

He looked oddly relieved. "Oh, well, Ellie, sweetheart, I didn't want to burden you with—"

"How long has she been like this?"

"Please, Ellie, don't raise your voice. She's finally sleeping and—"

"How long?"

"Well, it's on and off, you know. Some days she seems so normal I could just—"

"How *long*?"

"Uh, oh God—since September, basically."

This past September Mom had begged me not to go back to school. But I had gone anyway. And that's when she had snapped. The guilt I felt right then was so bruising it was as if that mugger had been able to hit me in the head with his stick after all.

My father followed me downstairs to the kitchen, talking the whole way, a constant murmuring stream as he pleaded with me not to leave. Ignoring him, I picked up the phone. I was going to call information, get the number for the local cab company. But I called Candace instead.

Except I got the machine, and even though I yelled for her to pick up, she didn't.

That terrified me, but I didn't have time to worry

189

about anyone else at the moment. Candace wasn't there for me. That was the main thing.

I took out my wallet. I found the number I wanted, dialed it. I got Ruth's machine. On it she gave her home number in case of emergency. I called that number next. I had to let it ring many times. My father was staring at me the whole time. I turned away.

"Hello?"

"Ruth, it's Ellie, I'm really sorry to wake you like this."

"Not at all, Ellie. Not at all. Oh dear. Wait a second, let me just get the bugs out of my brain, if you know what I . . . Are you okay?"

"No, I'm not."

"I'm sorry. What ails? Ellie?"

"I can't talk about it right now."

"Ah. Well, you know, Ellie, I have to wonder then why you are calling." She said it gently. It was the kind of joke that often delighted me in our sessions. But right now I was too far gone to smile.

"I can't talk about it right now," I repeated angrily.

There was a pause. "Where are you?" Ruth asked.

"I'm at home. In New Jersey."

"Ah, yes, I see."

"And my father is sitting right here staring at me, so it's kind of hard to talk. Dad, could you let me have some privacy? *Please?*"

Instantly, my father dropped his head into his hands and began to weep, which was a heartrending sight. Mom crying was a common sight for me. Mom not crying was something rarer. But Dad crying—that was rarest of all. I had only seen Dad cry twice, once when his brother died, and the first time Mom wouldn't come out of her room.

190

His head still down, Dad got to his feet and shuffled out of the room. I heard him crying in the den.

"What is happening, Ellie?" Ruth asked.

I had such a big lump in my throat I could barely get the words out.

"That was my father crying," I said.

"Yes," she said. "Why is he crying, please?"

"Something bad . . . happened."

"Yes. What, Ellie?"

"Oh, God, Ruth, help me! Please God help me!"

"I will try, Ellie. Now, if you would please tell me what—"

"Don't you see? There's no one I can trust anymore. No one. No one!"

"Ah. Well, you can trust me, Ellie."

I trusted her. I trusted her totally. "Oh, Ruth," I cried, "will you . . ."

I was going to say—"be my mother?" But even in my racked state I had enough self-control left to avoid saying the real request in its true naked form. ". . . will you take care of me?"

"As best I can, my sweet child. As best I can. But you know, Ellie, as I have told you before, you are taking care of yourself. Whether you know it or not."

"I'm *not!*"

"But you are, Ellie. And you've been doing it your whole life, you just have never given to yourself the credit for this."

She listened to me crying. Then said, "Ellie?"

"Y-yes?"

"It's hard for me to help you now over the phone like this if you won't tell me what it is that has happened. Is it something with your mom?"

". . . yes."

191

She waited. I couldn't speak.

Finally I said, "Can I come . . . see you?"

"Of course."

"Now?"

There was a pause.

"Yes of course, Ellie, but it is very late, you know. How would you get here?"

"I don't know. I guess I could take a cab."

"You have the money? A cab from Englewood is a pretty penny, yes?"

"Yes. I have the money."

"Okay, then. If you promise me you will take a cab and have this cab wait for you until you are inside the building . . ."

I promised. Ruth gave me her address. "I will tell the doorman to be waiting on you," she said.

And then we hung up.

CHAPTER 30

RUTH LIVED IN ONE OF THOSE BIG BEAUTIFUL old apartment buildings that line Riverside Drive like a row of castles. Hers was on Riverside and 109th.

My cabdriver was a kind-seeming Egyptian man who kept murmuring sympathetic-sounding words that I couldn't understand while I wept in the backseat. I was sure that he didn't understand a word I told him. But we got to the right address, so he must have understood part of what I said, and then he waited until I was safely inside, just as I had asked.

The uniformed doorman was sleeping on a little black stool inside the door when I came up. When I knocked he jerked awake and hurried to let me in. Then he buzzed Ruth's apartment. She came on the house phone almost instantly and told the doorman to please send me up.

The lobby was palatial, with marble floors and vaulted ceilings and fresh-cut flowers in vases on side tables. Even the mailboxes looked fancy—gleaming polished brass. The doorman pointed me to the farthest elevator. "Eleven-C," he said. As I got on the elevator I saw him climbing back on his stool and slipping back into sleep.

There were only two apartments on the eleventh floor, one on either end of a short hallway. In between was another table with flowers and a gilt-edged mirror in which I saw my face. I was stunningly pale, the whiteness attractively offsetting my red-rimmed eyes. And then, thanks to the mirror, I saw something else.

The service elevator, which was right next to the passenger elevator, had two signs taped over its gray metal doors—OUT OF SERVICE and WARNING! The doors were slightly open—showing a gaping blackness within. And right away my helpful mind provided me with dramatic footage of me fallllllling down that empty elevator shaft, spinning slowly through the air before—*Wham!*—I splatted dead on top of the elevator cage eleven floors below.

I looked away. Ruth's door was open. I went in.

It was a beautiful old apartment, filled with books and plants and old furniture and—

Maybe that's what did it. The furniture.

It was an old lady's furniture.

Not surprising. Ruth was an old lady. But for the first time since my first session, when I had been startled by the sight of Ruth at the door, I found myself thinking about Ruth's age. . . .

And the age of the killer they were looking for.

"I'm in the kitchen," Ruth called, "making us some Sleepytime tea, in honor of the hour, you know. Come in, come in, come in."

I stepped hesitantly into the living room, walking across the dark plush Oriental carpet, suddenly afraid that the rich paisley pattern might come to life like slithery snakes and grab me and pull me down.

I am losing my mind, I told myself.

"Sit down please," came the disembodied old voice, as if playing over a loudspeaker.

And then I thought about all those movies where the arch-villain speaks to the trapped hero at the start of the final showdown. The hero can't see the villain, only hear him, and usually the villain says something like, "So nice of you to join us here at the villa, Mr. Bond." And then the hero whirls around, gun in hand, and fires at the villain, but it turns out it's only a picture of the villain that he saw, or a mirror or—

In the kitchen, the kettle whistled. "Here we go," Ruth said.

I yelled at myself not to daydream, not to zone out on movies, not now! Because wasn't it possible, just possible, that my life was at stake, at this very moment? I stared hard at the living room, searching for clues. The high-ceilinged room was crowded with stuff—dark, depressing oil paintings that looked like they had all been done by the same painter (Ruth's dead husband?), a large Russian samovar, the complete works of Sigmund Freud, a condensed *Oxford English Dictionary* on its own wooden stand. Everything looked screamingly safe and familiar; the typical academic intellectual stuff I was so used to. But tonight everything that I was used to no longer seemed safe.

Then I noticed something else. Everything was spotless. No dust or dirt in sight, which was quite an accomplishment in a Manhattan apartment where soot flew in through the window every day like an alien invasion. And I thought about that profile Candace had read at the police station. . . .

The killer was highly organized. And what had Candace said?

Does that mean they live in a neat apartment?

"Hello, my dear," Ruth said kindly. "Let's sit over here by the window. It's cozy there."

She was wearing a dark red flannel nightgown and carrying a tray. Neatly arranged on the tray were a teapot, two mugs of steaming tea, and a tin of home-made brownies. Her old feet were bare. My eyes zoomed in on them, as if that somehow were particularly significant and scary—bare feet.

"I'm really sorry to wake you like this."

"Okay, yes," Ruth said, "for this you have already apologized. One apology to a customer, no?"

We sat. She stirred her tea. I didn't touch mine.

"Have some," she suggested.

Poison, I thought. I picked up the mug and held it, but I didn't take a sip. I looked out the window. "That's quite a view you have," I said, my voice sounding strange to me.

"Yes, I can see New Jersey. Perhaps I can even see your house from here. But I can't see what happened there, Ellie. This you must tell me."

I kept staring out the window. When I'd been crying on the phone with Ruth an hour ago, I'd felt like an open wound, like I could have told her my innermost thoughts without hesitation. But for one thing, I had cried myself out in the cab. I felt like a hollow shell with nothing left to tell. For another, I couldn't shake this crazy notion—

"Would it help if I would guess?" I heard Ruth say.

I didn't move.

"Your mother is suffering a psychotic episode, yes? She has become paranoid, no?"

196

I looked up slowly. Ruth was studying me with her usual kind gaze, but now that look struck me as pure evil. "How did you know that?"

"Ah, well, give me pats on the back, but you know, you patients always reveal a lot more than you think, and we are trained to read between the lines and—"

"Have you been out to my house?"

She reached across and put her hand on my arm. Her skin felt dry and leathery. "Ellie, I'm wrong to joke. It came as quite a shock to you, I am sure of this. A psychotic break is a horrible thing to witness."

I looked down at my cup of tea. I wanted to put it back down, but I was overcome by a wave of sadness as I remembered my mother in the kitchen, whispering about her conspiracy theories. I didn't think I could move. "I think I'm crazy, too," I said at last.

"No, you are not. You're just under a terrible strain."

"No, I think I am. It makes sense that I am. I mean, isn't this stuff genetic?"

"Partly. But we therapists think that environment plays a much bigger part than the genes."

"Then I am definitely crazy because—"

"No, you are not, you are not, and that is that. But I will tell you something. I will skip ahead to the end of our therapy, if you like, and give you, how you say? The answer in the back of the book? But."

She gave me a peculiar look.

"If I tell you this, you have to promise not to end your therapy with me, ha-ha. Because this, when patients terminate too soon before they are healthy, this I must admit is one of the few things that make me really furious."

She rapped her spoon sharply against the edge of

her mug, then set it down. "But, where was I? Yes. Sometimes lonely children, and you were a lonely child, Ellie, whether you like it or not—"

"My mother was always with me," I said almost by rote. "She didn't work. She was always home."

"Yes, but she couldn't really give to you the love you needed, because she just didn't have it to give. She was so unhappy, yes? That's why you were always watching the movies, movies, movies, because it was an escape."

"Movies as an escape, that's why everyone watches the—"

"Now, lonely children will go a very long distance to try to identify with their parents. They want to be like them, to be close to them. You follow this? That's why I think this fearful nature of yours—I don't think it's really you. I think, deep inside, Ellie, you are a much braver person than you give yourself credit for, but you stay in this fearful state as a way of— What? Why are you looking at me like that?"

"I just thought of something."

Which was true. I had just thought of something. But it was something I couldn't say.

"What?" she asked.

What I had thought was, Abby had just terminated her therapy with Ruth. And certainly she had ended therapy way before she was healthy. Ruth said that was one of the things that made her really mad.

And Jenny Silver—she was another patient of Ruth's. And then—

I thought of something else.

We were on 109th Street. What if Jenny had kept walking that night, searching for that stupid chocolate soda for her roommate—

What if she had walked a couple of blocks farther than Candace and I had walked—

She would have come to 109th Street.

And maybe she had run into—

"Ellie," Ruth said, "you really must start to talk to me. Or at least, please, have some of that tea. It's getting cold."

"I'm sorry," I said, standing up. "It was wrong of me to come here."

"Nonsense. You were totally right to call me. This was a good instinct. This was an instinct of survival."

Had she told that to Abby, too? And to Jenny? Right before she slit their throats with her dead husband's straight-edged razor?

"I have to go."

"Nonsense. You are going nowhere."

"Why? You can't stop me."

"What? You think I'm going to tie you to a chair? No, but you will sleep here, Ellie. It's four in the morning for goodness' sakes. There are three extra bedrooms. I rattle around in this apartment like a marble."

I took a step toward the door.

"Wait," she said.

I turned back.

"Let me throw some clothes on and I'll come with you."

"Why?"

"If you're going home I want to see you home. You are my patient, you know. That is like you are my child. I have a responsibility."

Was that how she did it? By pretending she had to see them home? And then, what? Push them down the empty shaft of the service elevator?

She disappeared down a long wide hallway and out of sight into one of the bedrooms. I stood, undecided. Half of me was screaming, Get out! Half of me was screaming, Stay!

I am losing my mind, I thought again. I am losing my mind. I am—

The mantra calmed me slightly.

"I truly hope you haven't left," Ruth called. She sounded old, frail, worried. "I'll just be a second, my dear."

Ruth as a murderer—it was utterly absurd. For the first time in hours I realized how exhausted I was.

Then I noticed I was still holding my untouched mug of tea. I looked toward the kitchen. I carefully walked the full mug of tea through the living room's open arch.

The kitchen was shockingly big and bright, with a checkerboard of black-and-white diamonds on the floor that made me dizzy. I dumped the tea in the big white sink. I needed something cold to drink. I opened the fridge.

There was plenty of food inside, but there was one item that caught my eye so strongly, it was as if the fridge were empty except for the—

Bottle of chocolate Yoo-Hoo.

Unopened.

Sitting by itself in the middle of the second shelf.

"You are hungry?" Ruth said from only inches behind me. "Perhaps this will satisfy you."

And then she plunged the knife deep into my back.

CHAPTER 31

I TURNED SLOWLY, LETTING THE FRIDGE swing shut behind me. I really had seen too many movies. I had to look at the empty kitchen twice before I believed I was really alone and that my fantasy of getting stabbed was just that—a fantasy.

I hurried out into the living room. I heard Ruth coming down the hallway. I ran to the door. Frantically I pressed the down button on the elevator, but someone had called it away to another floor. No time. I ran to the door to the stairwell and started down the stairs, splaying my feet outward like a duck so I could take the steps faster, faster.

Back on the eleventh floor I could hear Ruth calling for me. I didn't stop. I figured she would wait for the elevator, old lady that she was. I just had to beat the elevator to the lobby.

I did.

The lobby was empty. I flew past the doorman—who woke with a terrible start—and banged out the front door.

Out into the freezing night. Out onto the deserted street.

So I was back in my nightmare, running through Manhattan late at night, begging to be mugged or killed, as Agent Wilkins had said.

I ran down 109th Street, headed back toward Broadway. The street was well lit but utterly silent and deserted. There were patches of ice on the sidewalk and I slipped on one, crashing into a row of garbage cans. They went over with booms loud as thunder. I had scratched my hands. I didn't stop, just scrambled to my feet and kept running.

And when I hit Broadway I raced right out into the street without even looking to see if there were any cars coming—because I was praying for some cars. I hailed a taxi, my arms windmilling.

"Police," I gasped. "Take me to the police." And then I locked both doors.

I was at the police station for several hours. Candace met me there. It turned out she had been so alarmed by the abrupt way I hung up that she had gone to New Jersey to make sure I was okay. Taxis passing in the night, two roommates losing their life savings.

Candace said my dad was sick with worry and she made me call him. I told him I was home and I was fine and I promised I would call him again tomorrow. Before we hung up he cried a little more—which made four times in my life I had heard him do that.

When I had run out of Ruth's apartment, I had been sure in every cell of my body that she was the killer. But when I told a bleary-eyed detective why I thought my therapist was a serial killer, my reasons sounded a lot skimpier. Then Candace put her hand on my arm and said she also had a suspect she wanted checked out. It was only then that I remembered my own suspicions about my mother. It seemed so long ago. I was grateful that Candace presented my theory as her own. It would have made me sound berserk otherwise.

Candace kept her hand on my arm the whole time she told the detective about Mom, like a good nurse trying to soothe me while I got my injection.

Even though Candace presented my theory, I was sure we sounded ridiculous to the detective. Five in the morning. One says it's her shrink, the other says it's her friend's mother.

"You get this a lot, don't you?" I asked.

"I could show you a stack this high," the detective said with a weary grin. "We've gotten tips on every member of the Barnard and Columbia faculty, the entire security force, half of Columbia's graduate-school students . . . everyone but you two girls is a suspect, basically."

"We're sure we're right," Candace said.

"You're both right?" the detective said with a wink.

He told us to wait. Then he went back down the hall. Candace and I were back sitting on those same wooden benches. An hour later Agent Wilkins came in with several other men in trench coats, stamping snow off their shoes. Agent Wilkins looked at us and shook his head. Then he headed off into the station.

We waited some more. Finally, the same exhausted detective came down and sat on the bench next to us, staring into a mostly empty Styrofoam cup of coffee as if it contained what he was about to say.

"Yeah," he said finally, "it's not your shrink and it's not your mother. Which if you ask me, has got to be good news for you both."

"Why?" I asked. "I mean, not why is it good news but why, you know . . . ?"

"Leiter and Sanchez were not patients of Ruth's. For starters. This summer she visited her hometown in Russia for the first time in eleven years. So she was not even in Manhattan when Jenny Silver disappeared."

"And Abby?" Candace asked.

The detective gave her an annoyed look. "She says she was home that night and her doorman confirms this."

"So," I said, "Abby could have gone to see her."

"She could have," the detective said, "but I don't think you've been listening to me. We're pretty sure at this point that these cases are all linked, certainly Silver and Rovere are. From what Agent Wilkins tells us, the person we're looking for is going to fit, you know, put all the puzzle pieces together."

"Ruth was mad at Abby because she terminated therapy," I said.

"And so she terminated *her?*" the detective asked. "As a motive, I don't buy it. Oh, and one other thing. Your shrink loves Yoo-Hoo. Drinks several bottles a day."

He turned to Candace. "Did your friend here ever tell you that her mom was agoraphobic? You know, afraid to go out of the house?"

It was awful hearing that clinical name for one of my mother's many problems. My mom had gone out less and less these past few years, that was true; but I didn't like hearing yet another crazy term thrown at her. She was raving, wasn't that enough?

"She didn't have to go out of the house that often," Candace said. "Just four times."

The detective nodded. He gave me a concerned look. "Can I talk to you in private?" he asked.

"You could say it in front of Candace, whatever it is."

"Your mom was in some kind of fancy loony-bin rest home when Abby disappeared."

I gaped at him.

Then I remembered. All those nights I hadn't been able to speak to Mom, when Dad had made up excuses. Harrison Ford movie, my ass.

The way I had seen my mother act tonight, the idea of her spending a few days in the loony bin didn't shock me. It just made me feel more exhausted than I already was.

I stood up. "C'mon, Candace, let's go home and let this poor man do his job."

"Hey," the detective said as we were leaving, "this *is* my job."

"Now I won't even be able to go to Ruth," I said. I should have been sobbing, the way I felt, but no tears came. "I've lost that, too. I've lost her."

"Of course you can go to Ruth," Candace said. "You think she'll blame you for this? She's a therapist. She'll analyze what you did. She loves it when you mess up, shows all her theories about you are right."

We were sitting at the kitchen table drinking coffee, since it was too late to try to go to sleep anyway. Outside the windows the sooty black sky was magically changing to light grimy gray. The city sun was coming up.

"Do you think that that detective could be right?" I asked Candace.

"About what?"

"Do you think that if we found the person who is doing this, she would fit into all four cases like the last piece in a jigsaw puzzle?"

"Yeah, I do."

I sipped my coffee. "I do, too," I said, "but then I think that's just because I'm a mathematician's daughter."

"Which means what?"

"I secretly believe everything should be logical. Like numbers. You end up with an answer. It's right or it's wrong. But what if these four cases make no sense whatsoever? What if they're just four random acts of senseless violence? Isn't that what they're always saying on the news? Another act of senseless violence, another act of senseless violence."

"No. Even senseless violence has some logic to it," Candace said.

"Well, I know all about logic," I said. "It's my best subj—"

"Your best what?"

I didn't answer.

"Ellie, what are you doing?"

I was freezing, despite the hot coffee; lack of sleep does that to me. But right now I was on overdrive. I got out my black notebook, the notebook I'd been using to jot down all my thoughts on the four cases. I hunted for a pen, found one uncapped on the sofa (it had left a tiny black mark). I started sketching a grid.

"What's that?" Candace demanded.

"That's our neighborhood, the whole Barnard area. Now . . . here we are." I made a large black X.

"X marks the spot," Candace said.

"That's the Boot," I said. "That's us."

"Why don't you draw a little boot instead of an X?"

We were getting punch-drunk we were so sleepy. I giggled. "I can't draw a boot now because I already drew an X and there isn't any room."

"Whatever."

"And here's campus." I marked it with a C.

"This is cool," Candace said. "You're using set theory, huh?"

"Get that file of yours, wouldya?" I asked. "I want to see something."

Candace took out several well-worn manila folders containing all the notes and files she and her group had kept on the missing-persons cases. With Candace's help, I drew in the last known locations for all four missing girls, and marked dotted lines for the possible routes they had taken on the nights they disappeared. Then I drew circles around the dotted lines, adding a couple of blocks on either side as a margin of error.

"So what is this, anyway?" Candace asked over my shoulder.

"It's like those Venn diagrams they teach you in high school. I want to see where the sets overlap."

I was done. We both stared at the paper. One circle—Abby's—was separate from the others, with no overlap whatsoever. The other three had a small point of intersection.

Maybe it was just the way I had drawn my diagram.

And it was just a diagram, after all.

But the spot where the three circles intersected contained a large black X.

CHAPTER 32

"HUH," I SAID.

"Huh," Candace repeated.

"Well, how about that."

We stared at each other. Abruptly, I shoved back from the table and stood, my chair tipping over behind me, the notebook falling to the floor.

"You're not going to say I'm the killer, are you?" Candace asked with genuine fear in her eyes.

"Molly," I said.

"Ellie," Candace began.

But I snapped my fingers, several times, fast and hard. "Molly. It's Molly."

"It's not, Ellie, I was—"

"Her apartment, her basement prison down there. It's so neat. Just like you said. Remember? It's an organized killer."

"Ellie, you're not listening to me. Don't you remember—"

"And way down there in the basement, who's going to hear somebody scream? There aren't even any windows." I was pacing. "Her mother whipped

208

her when she was little. That's bound to make you nuts. My mother didn't hit me and I'm nuts, imagine what Molly must be like."

"Molly is a rock."

I glanced at her, then went on pacing, circling around the kitchen and back into the living room like a restless zoo bear. "That first night, the first night when I was down there, I got this very creepy feeling. What's that saying? First instincts are always right? I'm telling you, if you hadn't come by just then, I think I would have been victim number four, instead of Abby."

"Ellie, of course you got a creepy feeling. You get a creepy feeling every day and so do I, because there's a killer on the loose. But you're forgetting something. I was downstairs talking to Molly the night Abby disappeared. I was down there for hours. I'm her alibi, for God's sake. And you still don't have a motive."

I let out a moan of frustration. I grabbed my notebook. I started writing again. LAUREN, I wrote, then drew a line across the page. MELITA. Another line. JENNY. ABBY.

"Now what?" Canace asked.

"I'll chart it."

"You'll what?"

"Like a logic problem. I'll chart the information. Read to me from those files."

"Ellie . . ."

"Read to me!"

Candace started reading, and whenever she came to a key word or phrase that sounded important to me, I jotted it down under the appropriate girl's name. I wrote down hometowns (Boca Raton, Riverdale, Cedarhurst, Brooklyn). I wrote down hobbies

209

(pottery, dressmaking, troll-doll collecting, moviegoing).
I wrote down sports, I wrote down clubs, I wrote
down majors. I wrote, I wrote, I wrote. Then I went
through and started circling words that appeared
more than once.

After much searching, I had circled *popular* three
times. There were circles under every girl but Abby.

I had circled *boyfriend* three more times—under
every girl but Abby.

"No pattern," Candace said, looking at what I had
done.

I chewed on the eraser. "Abby's an outlier," I said.

"A what?"

"It's a statistics term. I learned it last year in
Peretzky's seminar. If there's one piece of data that
deviates too far from the norm, you just chuck it out.
Abby doesn't fit, so we ignore her."

"Oh, that's convenient. Remind me never to trust
statistics."

"And"—I hurried on—"if we leave her out there's a
definite pattern. These girls who were killed, they all
had boyfriends. Oh, wow."

I gulped. Then I reached out with both hands and
clutched Candace's bare arms.

"What?" she whispered, catching my terror.

"I've got it." I turned and stared all around the
apartment. Then I got up and raced around opening
closet doors. Candace was running around after me,
obviously afraid that I had had a psychotic break of
my own. But that night I had had my own mother spy
on me from the shadows, and I was suddenly convinced that we were not alone in the apartment.

We were.

"It's Molly," I said, barely breathing the words.

210

We were back in the living room. "Ellie, we've been through thi—"

Candace started talking in her normal confident loud voice. I stopped her mouth with my hand. Shook my head.

"It's Molly," I repeated. "What does she say about boyfriends? They're bad. Being with boys—it's bad, bad, bad. So—she punishes girls who are popular."

"No."

"Yes. Look—that chart of mine shows that all those girls went walking in this general vicinity on the night they disappeared. Now, how did she lure them here? She—"

I had that answer, too. The revelations were coming so fast my skin was icy.

"She walks her dog at midnight," I said. "It's on her schedule. She walks Bert. Up and down the block. Patrolling. That means she's down by Broadway. Jenny could have run into her that night. So could the rest of them."

"Not Abby."

"She's an outlier, I'm telling you. Now, what happens when she runs into them? Do they know her?"

"Jenny did."

I started to sweat. Cold waves. "What are you talking about?"

"Jenny and I were both over here lots of times visiting Alexandra and Penny. Jenny knew Molly. Liked her, too."

"Why didn't you tell me?"

"I didn't think of it. It wasn't important—isn't important. You still haven't—"

"Leiter and Sanchez probably knew her, too."

"Oh, that's a leap."

211

"Not really. Molly's famous around here. Everyone loves Molly."

"Which proves she's a killer."

"'Never trust anyone but yourself,'" I said. "Candace Burkett. Quote unquote."

"And Molly. Trust Molly."

"Why? She's the big exception?"

"Yes. Ellie, you can stop with the scary looks. I trust Molly. I admit it. Give me a break."

"Someone we trust," I said, letting the words echo eerily. "It was in the fax."

Candace gave out a long exasperated sigh. "But what about Abby?"

I pointed at Candace angrily. "Stop fighting me!"

"I'm sorry, but I don't think you're right."

"Well, pretend like you do, just for a second, because I'm on a roll, in case you didn't—" I yanked on my hair with both hands. "I've got it!"

"Got what?"

"Abby told Molly that she and Seth were getting married."

"Now, why would she do that?"

"Because," I said, "she was depressed. That last time I talked to her? She told me that Seth had proposed marriage. She wanted me to believe it, too. Let's say she told Molly the same thing, and Molly killed her before she had a chance to explain. Or Molly started to kill her and then didn't believe her when Abby said she'd been lying about Seth. Or . . ."

Candace was waving her hands like semaphore flags. "I. Was. With. Molly. The. Night. Abby. Disappeared."

That stopped me. I felt the wind go out of my sails, felt all my brain power go slack.

"What's your answer to that, Ellie? We killed her together?"

No.

My answer to that was . . .

That I didn't have an answer.

I held my head in my hands.

I thought I had had it—and now it was gone.

I had no idea who the killer was.

CHAPTER 33

IT TOOK SEVERAL HOURS, BUT I FINALLY wound down and slept. I slept all day. There was so much I was afraid of right now, I think my body was drugging itself as a safety precaution. I came out of my room at around eight the next evening, and there was Candace sitting at the table going over her notes on the case. And my notes. Working away.

"Hey," she said.

"Hey. You got anything?"

"Not yet."

"You close to getting anything?"

"Just shut up, wouldya, and let me think? And by the way, I haven't forgotten that you said I wasn't logical the other night. I am logical. When I want to be."

I smiled. "And I thought you never carried grudges."

The phone rang. I jumped, of course. These days every sudden sound scared me. (As opposed to the era before the campus serial killer, when I was brave and fearless.)

Candace answered. "Oh, hi," she said, like she knew the caller. She chatted for a while, then held the phone out to me and said, "It's for you."

I raised my eyebrows; she shrugged.

"Hello?"

"Ellie, it's Stuart Englander."

I had to think for a moment before I remembered who that was.

"Oh, yeah. Listen, Stuart, I'm sorry we accused you the other night, but you gotta admit, the coincidence—"

"Forget it," he said.

That was big of him.

"Seriously? You're not mad?"

"I was, I'm over it. It's history."

"Thanks."

"So. Listen. Since I scared the heck out of you in the library the other night, I thought I ought to, you know, make it up to you. How about dinner?"

"How about what?"

"Dinner. You know, as in food we eat together. Maybe at a restaurant. I know this place, Pancho Villa, that serves wicked nachos."

"Is this a joke?"

"What do you mean?"

"You're asking me out to eat?"

Candace was making all kinds of suggestive gestures. I swatted at her, but she danced away.

"Look, I know that time in September . . . that was pretty awkward, 'cause I was there to ask Candace out—I guess you figured that out. Yeah, Grady figured that out, too, by the way, and we almost ended our friendship. But that's all blood under the bridge, as they say. So whatta you say, though, do we have a date or don't we?"

"Have you been in a foreign country?"

"Does L.A. count?"

"I'm serious. Do you know what's going on here? Do you know about Abby?"

215

"Yeah . . . that's awful. I hope she's okay."

"I mean, most of the campus is going home," I told him. "In case you didn't notice."

"No, yeah, I know. You're brave to stick around, by the way; I like that."

That's right. I wasn't going home. Not me. I was too busy accusing every old woman in Manhattan of being a serial killer.

"Waitttt a minute," I said. "I get it."

"Get what?"

"I know why you're calling. You think if you take me out a couple of times, you can get back on track with Candace."

I had been through this degrading strategy with several of Candace's suitors.

"No way," he said, sounding only mildly offended.

"It won't work."

"Ellie," he said. "You're paranoid."

That hurt, like a dentist's drill boring into my weakest spot.

"Go to hell," I said.

He sighed. "Well," he said, "this phone call sure is going well. Look," he said, "I swear to you I'm not calling you 'cause of Candace. If you want to know the absolute truth, I do feel a little bad about scaring you in the library that night. See, I saw you hunting around in the stacks. So I stuck my face through the shelf like that just to spook you. I didn't know it would work so well."

"And you call me paranoid." But I laughed. Not because what he said was so funny, but because he had begun to convince me that he was after me, not Candace. That idea made me so happy I *had* to laugh.

"You have got the world's weirdest timing," I said.

"Thanks," he said.

216

Last night had been such a horror show, I was expecting to wake up in hell. Instead, here was something that excited me and made my heart sing. Nothing could have confused me more.

"Okay, you can tell me," Stuart said. "Us going to dinner is a stupid idea, right? Go ahead. Just say, 'It's a stupid idea,' and I'll hang up."

Candace was glaring at me, waving at me, giving me every possible kind of signal, and every signal meant for me to say—

"Yes," I said. "I mean, not yes it's a stupid idea but yes, let's go get something to eat. That's exactly what I need. I've been so wired lately that . . ."

So twenty minutes later I found myself wearing fresh eyeliner and blush and lip gloss and tromping down to the frozen street to meet Stuart Englander, my first date of the year.

Molly was outside, looking even bigger than usual since she was bundled into her thick old brown hooded overcoat. I had wondered in the fall what snow would do to Molly and her strict schedule. I had long ago found the answer. Nothing. She added a shovel and a bucket of salt to her routine, making sure that the front of the building was neat and ice-free throughout the winter. But other than that, she did everything the same. She still kept her broom, too, and after she was done shoveling and salting, she did some token sweeping. Not real cleanup sweeping, more like she was just jabbing at the ground as she walked around muttering to herself.

Right now she was jabbing the broom in the direction of Stuart, who was laughing and holding his arms up in the air as if the broom were a gun. He kept dodging backward.

"Why do you have to keep messing around my building?" Molly demanded. "How come?"

"Old Molly doesn't think we ought to go to dinner," Stuart called to me.

"It's okay, Molly," I said. "Really."

"It's not okay," she grumbled, but she let Stuart go. As she trundled past me I saw a shocking sight. Old Molly was wearing lipstick.

"Hey, now," I said. "Maybe I'm not the only one with a date tonight."

Molly gave me such a hurt look I immediately regretted teasing her. "That's right, go ahead and laugh," she said.

And then I saw him. Fred. I knew it was him way before I should have been able to recognize him, because he was shuffling along in a thick overcoat of his own, and I hadn't laid eyes on him too often. But I knew. Uh-oh, I thought. We're in for it now.

Molly had seen him, too. She glanced at me guiltily. I tried to smile in a way that would put her at ease and make up for teasing her.

"Ellie?" Stuart said. "Can we go?"

"Yeah."

But I didn't move, just stayed where I was, mesmerized by Fred's approach.

There was something under his arm, hanging down loosely because he had his hands stuffed deep in his pockets. It was only when he came closer that I could make out what he was carrying—a bouquet of frozen roses.

"Go on now," Molly told us. "Get away now. Leave us be."

I took a few steps toward Stuart, but I couldn't help it, I looked back.

218

Fred glanced at me, looking as furtive and guilty as Molly. He looked different, even thinner than usual, almost skeletal. Then I realized why. He had shaved off his beard. Why? In honor of the date?

I waited for Molly to start shouting and waving her broom at Fred. Instead, she threw me one more fearful look, then turned and walked into the Boot without looking back. Fred shuffled after her, moving the rose bouquet back and forth between his bare frozen hands.

Then they were gone.

Another piece of my theory had shattered into bits. Molly obviously didn't think men were as bad as she said. So where was her motive now?

I turned and was almost surprised to see Stuart standing there. He burst out laughing. "Good evening," he said, bowing grandly.

Actually, I think that the strange drama of Molly and Fred had helped break the ice—and not the ice on the sidewalk, the ice between me and Stuart. From that moment on, it was like we couldn't stop talking. None of those long yawning date silences that I dreaded so much. Stuart, as it turned out, was into movies as much as I was. Okay, he was into current movies mainly, not like me and Mom, who loved the oldies. But his favorite movie of all time was *Casablanca* ("Mine, too!") and he hated colorization. *And* . . . he was writing a screenplay (well, who wasn't writing a screenplay?) though he wouldn't tell me what it was about.

"Is that stupid?" he said, wiping nacho grease from his lips not with his yellow cloth napkin but with his hand. "I mean, like who's going to steal my idea? Like my idea is so hot that someone is going to take it, right? But still, I don't know, I'm superstitious, I guess. And anyway, it *is* a fabulous screenplay."

He went on to tell me that that was the reason he'd flown back home to L.A., to meet with his rich movie-producer Uncle Roddy and peddle the idea. His uncle was reading the script this week, supposedly.

"Should I just tell you the idea?" he asked.

I actually didn't want him to tell me the idea, and I said so. Though I didn't tell him *why* I didn't want to know the idea. What if it was lousy? Then how would I respect him? This way, I could just imagine that his script was brilliant (though not as brilliant as the screenplays I would write, of course), and go on making goo-goo eyes at him across the tiny table in the dark grotto that was Pancho Villa. Which is what I did.

Fifteen minutes later I was already very tipsy from the large frozen margarita Stuart had ordered for me. The only other time I could remember feeling this buzzed was the last date I'd had with Stuart—the fake date—when I'd drunk all that wine.

But this was a real date. And now we had begun that ritual of all excellent first dates, the swapping of life stories. I left out my latest headlines, of course, that my mother had gone insane. Stuart told me all about his lonely adolescence in Houston, Texas, of all places. His father, a geologist who hunted for oil for Exxon, had taken custody of Stuart after his mother died, and those years with Dad had been the worst years of Stuart's life. Before that, he had lived alone with his mom in Boca Raton. Which, he admitted, hadn't been such great years either.

Stuart alone with his mother in Florida, Grady polishing his glasses in Charleston, Molly with her schedule in New York—secretly everyone was miserable and crazy, I thought. It made me feel a little better about poor Mom. And it made me like Stuart more.

Or maybe it was just that I was now extremely tipsy—or maybe even drunk—from my second large frozen margarita, which the waiter brought without my ever asking.

And then I had a third margarita, which just magically appeared on the table before me after I had slurped the last of the second. Or was that the fourth?

Then we were outside again. I stumbled around on the ice a little outside the restaurant, which meant Stuart had to hold me up, which I didn't mind one bit. We ended up in front of one of the big Columbia dorms. I stared up at it strangely. "Grady lives here," I said sagely. My entire brain was spinning like my mother's dishwasher in its final furious cycle.

"Yes," Stuart said with a laugh. "Grady is my roommate."

"That's right," I said.

Stuart suggested I come up to his room for a while to hang out. I agreed. This seemed like a sensible idea.

There was an old-woman security guard on duty at the downstairs desk of his dorm. Age had shrunken her cheeks and given her a V-shaped hawklike face. She studied us in the security camera. Stuart held up his ID card and she buzzed us in. She was giving us dirty looks the whole time we waited for the elevator, and I was giving her dirty looks right back, for reasons of my own.

We walked into the living room of a two-bedroom suite. The living room was decorated on one side with posters of models in bathing suits (and less) and on the other side with framed, stately black-and-white photographs of Charleston, South Carolina. There seemed to be two of everything: two CD players, two bookcases, two lamps. It was like looking at a before-and-after picture. One side of the room—the side I knew in

221

a glance was Stuart's side—was terribly messy with dirty clothes strewn everywhere. The other side, Grady's side, was ridiculously neat, with all the furniture and belongings arranged at perfect right angles. Painted down the middle of the room was a thin black line.

And sitting smack in the middle of what I was sure was Stuart's side—was Grady. He was wearing only an old pair of jockey briefs and his ever-present wire-rim glasses. He was sitting on a metal folding chair, trimming the cuticle of his big toe with a pair of nail clippers. He was letting the dead nail bits drop onto the floor.

"You're on my side of the room again, Grady," Stuart told him quietly.

"Hi, Grady!" I said.

Grady grabbed for a towel that hung on a nearby closet doorknob. "Ellie!"

"So this is what you do when I'm not around, eh, Grady?" said Stuart. "And you're always complaining I'm such a slob. You're going to sweep that up, you hear me?"

Grady glared at Stuart. "I figured you wouldn't notice a little more mess."

"Yeah, well, I forgive you," Stuart said, "just don't do it again."

"We're drunk," I said loudly. "Or at least I am."

Clutching the towel around his waist, Grady hurried into his bedroom, but not before giving Stuart a piercing look.

"Grady's pissed," Stuart confided in a whisper.

"Why?" I whispered back. I really couldn't imagine. "He was the one on your side of the living room."

"Yeah, but he's been talking about asking you out lately."

"He *has?*"

222

I had already been feeling extremely woozy; now I almost fainted dead away.

"Yeah. He finally gave up on Candace, you know."

"Well that's good. I mean, he should, as a girl-friend, anyway."

"Yeah. So then he was saying he was going to ask you out."

"Well, why didn't he?"

"It takes Grady forever to do anything. Like he still hasn't totally forgiven me for trying for Candace myself. That's when our little war started. That's when he painted this line."

He toed the line with his sneaker.

"It was supposed to be a joke," Stuart said, "but it hasn't been much of a joke lately. He hates me."

The topic of roommate wars didn't interest me when there was this other astounding topic on the table. "So," I said, "why did you ask me out if he was going to?"

Stuart shrugged. "I already told you. I felt sorry for scaring you in the library."

I didn't like that answer. It made me think of my earlier theory about why Stuart had asked me out. Which was . . . That's funny, I thought. I could no longer remember my own theory.

"This is my bedroom over here," Stuart said.

The decor in his room was like an extension of his side of the living room, but in here his slob style was on display in its purest form. There were more sexist bimbo posters slapped to the walls and more dirty clothes on the floor and, somewhere in there, a naked mattress and a desk piled high with papers.

"Please excuse appearances, but the maid quit," Stuart said.

"You're not a neat person, are you?"

223

"You must be a detective."

"No," I said. "I'm not a detective. Detective Pearl is a detective. But I'm not."

Stuart guided me across a minefield of empty pizza boxes, books, sneakers, and dumbbells to his unmade bed. He sat me down on the mattress. He started kissing me flush on the lips.

"Grady's very neat," I said, pulling my head back. It wasn't that I wasn't into the kiss—which felt astonishingly good. But I was so drunk that right in the middle of the kiss I sort of forgot we were making out.

"Yes, he is neat," agreed Stuart. "In fact, you might even go so far as to say Grady is insanely neat."

"Maybe Grady is a killer," I said.

"Maybe he is."

"What are you doing?"

"Unzipping your coat."

"Why are you unzipping my coat?"

"Because we're inside now and you must be hot. Aren't you hot?"

"I am a little hot."

"Then that's why I'm doing it."

"Is that why you're taking off my sweater?"

"Uh-huh. Lift your arms up. That's it. Good."

"Stuart?"

"Yes?"

"Why are you unbuttoning my blouse?"

"Same reason, you know, as with the coat and the sweater."

"I don't think so. I think it's a different reason. I think it's a different reason altogether."

"You know what, Ellie? You got me there."

I again lifted my hands cooperatively as he removed my blouse.

224

Just then, there was a knock at the door. Grady coughed. We looked up. And from some distant sober corner of my inebriated mind I noted something odd. The odd thing was, even though I was sitting here with my shirt off, I wasn't at all embarrassed.

"Hi, Grady," I said.

"Can I talk to you for a second, Stuart?"

"Yeah, sure. Ellie? I'll be right back, okay?"

"Okeydokey."

Stuart closed the door behind him, but I could still hear them arguing outside.

"I don't really understand this, Stuart," Grady said. And then something about how it was Candace all over again . . . and after that something about me being really plastered and decent behavior around women.

I got up, teetered sharply, and pitched back down at Stuart's desk. Made it! I ran my fingers over the keyboard of his computer. So this was where he wrote his almost-as-brilliant-as-my-screenplay screenplays. I thought of turning on the computer and spying on his work-in-progress. It was the kind of thing Candace would have done. It was the kind of thing I could brag to her about later, to show her that Candaceness was indeed rubbing off on me, that the transformation of scaredy-cat Ellie Sommers into a tough New Yorker was proceeding apace. But then I saw the screenplay itself.

There was a thick black ringbinder lodged underneath a pile of papers. That had to be the screenplay. I reached for it.

All the papers on top of the binder fell with a fluttering crash as I pulled the binder out from underneath.

"Whoops," I said.

I looked toward the door, but Stuart didn't come

back in. I could hear them arguing more loudly now.

I opened the binder.

FBI ADMITS POSSIBLE LINKAGE FOR MISSING BARNARD GIRLS

It was a clip from the *Spectator*, carefully positioned inside the plastic page. So Stuart was a slob about some things and not about others.

Hmm . . . I thought. I wonder why Stuart is clipping articles on the case.

I turned the page.

BARNARD GIRL MISSING

It was the front page article from *The New York Times* that had caused my mother and father such worries this past September. It was strange to see it again, a snapshot of a moment in my life that now seemed light-years, not months, away.

I studied the photo of Jenny Silver, a face now more familiar to me from the flyers around town than from real life. The notebook was heavy in my hands. A word popped into my head.

Souvenirs.

FBI TO HELP WITH STRING OF PROSTITUTE KILLINGS

This clip was from L.A., Stuart's current hometown. A series of unsolved murders . . . serial killer suspected . . . and then part of a line was underlined. . . .

" . . . *in some cases the bodies have not been found* . . ."

I leaned my head close to the page, studying the small print. The dates of the murders . . . that was strange . . . they seemed to coincide with summer or Christmas break or spring break . . . times that Stuart would have been home—

I flipped the page.

CHAPTER 37

THE HALLWAY WAS NARROW, MOLLY WAS large. There was no way to get around her. I tried anyway, but I ended up just running right into her arms.

I felt my eyes roll back, felt my limbs go weak. I think I threw up on her old gray sweater.

I was going in and out of consciousness then . . . but I was aware of being dragged . . . out into the hall. . . .

Something swung open. I heard metal creaking. Then I saw it up close. The garbage chute. I saw a little orange scrap of carrot that had fallen out of someone's garbage and stuck to the metal. And then Molly pulled me back a few inches and I was staring at that little label that warns you not to throw anything flammable down into the incinerator and then—

Molly rammed my head right down into the black hole. And I stuck there. I felt her shoving from behind, trying to squeeze me in. I kept my hands outside. She was prying them off, stuffing them back in the chute, trying to turn me to fit me in. I started to kick.

Candace's cowboy boots came in handy one more

time, because I felt my boot connect with something and I heard Molly grunt. For a second Molly wasn't holding me, wasn't shoving me. I pushed myself out of the chute, fell to the ground.

Molly pounced on me, her hands grabbing my hair. I wriggled. I got away, all except my head. She was pulling me back by my hair. I screamed and brought my legs up, bicycling them to kick up at her face.

I didn't reach that far, but I kicked her arms and she let go of my hair.

I scooted forward, then got up, then charged at the stairs.

I fell down the first flight, tumbling, hands, legs, head knocking against the steps and the banister. When I came to a stop, my head bashed into the banister one more time. I felt something crack, maybe the wood of the banister, maybe my skull.

Molly was charging down the steps toward me. I dragged myself to my feet and stumbled on, around the hall to the next landing and down, down, down.

She was far enough behind me as I came down the front steps that I could have made it out the front door. But it was another one of those crossroads. And I was running so fast that luckily I didn't have more than a split-second to think about it. So all I needed was one fraction of an instant of bravery and loyalty and I had it because—

I turned the corner past the front door and kept running down to the basement, down into the inferno, down to Candace.

The door to Molly's apartment was closed, but when I yanked, it opened, and I raced in. I headed straight for the bathroom, that closed door, with Bert barking and jumping at me.

I pulled open the bathroom door.

Empty.

Spotless.

Gleaming faucets.

Dripping tap.

Drip, drip, drip.

And in the sink, down by the drain, sat something silver. I looked closer. It was a mermaid ring, the figure's long silver hair wreathed around in a circle so that it blended in with her fishy tail. The ring that Candace could never slip off her finger.

The ring was wet. But still clinging to the silver were a few drops of blood.

I stepped back and looked down. There were more red droplets on the otherwise spotless floor, a red trail of droplets like one of the dotted lines on my Venn diagram of the victims' last routes. I followed the trail.

It led me back out the door. Bert nipped at my heels, barking, barking.

I didn't see Molly as I came out into the dark hot basement. It was hard to look for her and follow the trail of blood at the same time. The trail led straight to—

The incinerator.

I pulled open the little metal door, searing my flesh on the handle.

Then I screamed.

A burned human arm had fallen out of the fiery furnace toward me, as if in greeting.

Dangling at the end of that arm was a hand, badly charred.

The hand was missing its ring finger.

CHAPTER 38

I DIDN'T EVEN HAVE TIME TO SCREAM.
Molly's belt buckle smacked me in the head. I fell
forward, banging my head against the burning-hot
incinerator, then slumped to the ground.

I was still conscious. I watched Molly raise her belt
over her head. Saw her swing down. The next lash
caught me in the thigh. Then she hit my forearm,
which I had draped over my face.

"Bad! Molly is bad!" she was shouting. Whipping me
again and again and—

Bert was barking wildly. Then there was a horrified
yowl. She turned on him, whipping him instead of
me.

That didn't last long. Bert ran for it.

I couldn't move. Even though my back felt like it
was blistering from the heat of the incinerator.

Molly hit me a few more times. Then she threw the
belt aside, disappearing into the darkness. She returned
quickly with her large metal shovel. She lifted it with
both hands.

Then she swung.

Though I didn't move an inch, she missed my head. She sliced the blade of the shovel deep into my shoulder, though. The metal shovel sparked against the incinerator.

And then she brought the shovel back up for the final blow.

CHAPTER 39

I HEARD A LOUD CRACK. BUT IT WASN'T THE sound of the shovel hitting the incinerator. Molly straightened, her mouth curling in a surprised sneer. She slowly sank to her knees, one big hand resting on my knee as gently as if we were still close friends.

Agent Wilkins ran forward, gun still drawn.

"Candace . . ." I said.

I didn't need to tell him. Candace's burned arm was dangling down, right over my head. Agent Wilkins peered into the incinerator. "Oh God in heaven." He looked as if he was going to be sick.

Finally he looked back down at me. He answered the question in my eyes.

"She's dead, Ellie."

I started to sob. He pulled Molly away from me, knelt down, and held me. "Poor girl," he said. He said it over and over.

But it wasn't comforting.

No one could comfort me ever again.

"I need . . . please . . . ambulance . . ."

He nodded. But he didn't make a move to use his walkie-talkie.

Just kept looking at me, this terrible pity in his eyes.

"C'mon," he said. "Let's get you away from that heat."

He moved me gently, carefully, half-sliding me, half-lifting me, until I was leaning against the wall. He inspected my shoulder wound, delicately lifting my sweater and peering inside.

"You're going to need stitches."

He held my chin almost tenderly, turning my head this way and that as he studied my bruises. "She gave you quite a beating."

My mind was barely working. But to the extent that I was thinking at all, I was trying to figure out why he was moving so slowly. Maybe he had already called for the ambulance. Yesssss, that was it. He called for the ambulance before he even came over here, so now he was just trying to keep me calm before the help arrived. . . .

"Does this hurt?" he asked.

He had found a bruise on my rib cage where the belt buckle had hit home. I moaned. "Yeah. Hurts." But he kept pressing down with his hand.

"I think there are some broken ribs," he said.

I was going to pass out if he didn't stop pressing down on my rib cage.

"Please . . ."

He let go.

But now he put his hands around my neck.

I stiffened, which was about all I had the strength left to do. He smiled. "Relax, I just want to make sure your neck isn't—" His smile broadened. "You're okay."

That wasn't how I felt.

251

And then it hit me.

What was going on.

"I'm going to die," I said.

He looked surprised. "Now, why do you say that?"

"You're just trying to make me feel better because you know there's nothing you can do."

"Nonsense. You're pretty badly nicked up, but you'll live."

"No, I won't."

"Sure you will," he said.

There was a gleam in his eye as he said it.

And then something passed between us, from his eyes to mine and back again.

"You know, don't you?" he said.

CHAPTER 40

"NO," I SAID.

And it was true. I didn't know what he was talking about.

"Abby," he said.

"Abby?"

Agent Wilkins still had his hands around my neck. He let go, squatted on his haunches, staring down at me. "You're a smart girl, Ellie, I'll give you that."

Not as smart as he thought.

"Abby?" I said again.

Agent Wilkins studied my face. Then he reached down and pressed down on my rib cage with the flat of his hand, pressing down twice as hard as before. My head flopped over. I spat up blood.

It was only when he let go that the pain subsided enough for me to scream.

"You know," he repeated.

"I don't!"

He watched me a moment more. Then he laughed. "You poor girl," he said. "And here I thought you had figured it out. Oh, well." He laughed again. "Now it's as good as if you had figured it out, because it's like I confessed, now, isn't it?"

He held my chin, gave it a little shake. "Isn't it."

I tried to move my head away, but I couldn't move at all.

He let go of my chin. He knelt down next to me, just watching me, as if I were an interesting specimen. I could feel the blood oozing out of my shoulder. My life was leaking away.

"You didn't . . . confess," I said lamely. "I don't know . . . a thing."

"Oh, now." He smiled. "Crime of opportunity, Ellie. That's what I kept telling you. She was coming back from the library. . . ."

"No, please, I don't want to know."

"She was coming back from the library—you girls were right about that."

"Please . . . "

"Oh," he said kindly, "you might as well know now. You earned it in a way. And I don't get to talk about it much." He dabbed at the sweat beading his forehead with a crisply ironed handkerchief from his pocket. Then he started wiping the sweat from my forehead as well . . . folding over the handkerchief again and again so that each time he touched me with a clean part of the cloth.

"I was cruising in my car, patrolling. I spotted her, told her to get in, told her it wasn't safe for her to be out walking late at night like that. No one saw us, of course. If they had, I wouldn't have done a thing, just driven her home.

"But instead I gave her some coffee from my thermos. Plus a little chloral hydrate that I had mixed in. Sleeping pills. Same stuff Molly served you in her

254

broth. Then I took her back to my vacation house upstate and put her in the wood-burning stove.

"That's what I do, Ellie. When I catch a serial killer, I hold off a little before turning them in. Oh, yeah, I knew it was Molly. I've known for several weeks now.

"Once I've caught the killer, then I wait for my chance. Wait for a golden opportunity. Anything less than that, I walk away. And you want to know the best thing? I'm never going to be caught. Never. See, I always use the same MO as the real killer. That way, when the serial killer is arrested and confesses to eleven murders instead of twelve, the FBI just assumes the psycho is being modest, that he's guilty of all twelve. They close the files, and I go on to the next case."

"I . . . really don't know what . . . what you're talking about. I'm . . . delirious. If you could just call an ambulance—"

His face clouded over. "I know what you're thinking. You're thinking it's wrong of me, what I do. But. You don't know what it's like, chasing serial killers. You have to get in the killer's head. And that means you have to find the killer in yourself. You understand?"

"No . . . I swear . . ."

"I'm an organized man. Methodical. I cover *every* angle. Study every clue. Every detail."

Every detail—like the glove compartment in his car, so neatly arranged. Everything at right angles.

Every detail—like how he would kill me next and get away with it.

I knew then that I was going to die.

"You're . . . a killer," I said. It was all I had left, my hatred for the man. I could leave him with that.

"Oh, yeah," he said. "Sure. I've killed a few people, sure. But it's all been in the line of duty. Part of the research, is what it is. And, listen now, I always catch the real killer. Always. That's what you're forgetting. I catch the killer, Ellie."

He held my hand. He started gently stroking the skin with his thumb.

"You know what I've found? You know what it all comes down to? It's about power, Ellie. Power. Simple as that. Take you, for instance. You looked up to me. I saw that from the first second we met. You put your *life* in my hands. Like a gift. And . . . well . . . now I'm taking it."

He sat in silence for a few more seconds. Smiled slightly. "Well. I think it's time."

It was. Molly, her gray sweater now drenched with blood, brought the shovel down with a dull thud against the back of his skull.

CHAPTER 41

HE WENT DOWN. HE GOT UP. THEY FOUGHT. I watched helplessly, as if I were sitting in the front row of my very last movie.

It wasn't a long fight. Molly had lost a lot of blood. She would have had to kill Wilkins with that first shot, and she didn't. He pulled the shovel out of her hands, tossed it aside. Then he kicked her, slapped her, tripped her, and down she went. She was a large old woman and the fall itself would probably have been enough to disable her. But he fell on top of her.

I watched as he choked her to death.

Molly squirmed and flailed around. Her head ended up on my lap. And that's where it was when she died, her eyes staring up at me with a sort of blank surprise.

When he finished choking her, Agent Wilkins gave me a similar look of surprise.

That was because, while he choked her I had taken his gun.

And now I fired. . . .

257

CHAPTER 42

THE RECOIL FROM THE GUN RAPPED MY head back against the cement basement wall. Agent Wilkins grunted and sat down, falling back on his bum.

His eyes were fixed on mine, but his hand was opening his coat.

Inside I saw the thick blue padding of his bulletproof vest.

And in his shoulder holster sat another shiny metal gun.

I fired again. This time I aimed right between his eyes. The force of the shot knocked my head back again. My hand was burning.

I must be the world's worst shot. Because even shooting from point-blank range, I missed Agent Wilkins's head completely.

I hit his shoulder instead. His hand swung away from the gun. I kept firing. And firing. Until I was out of bullets and Agent Wilkins was lying on his back, arms at his sides, legs bloody where I had shot him three times.

*   *   *

I suppose that in some ways it's lucky that I didn't kill Agent Wilkins, but with all my heart I wish I had.

But then again, if I had killed him, who knows if anyone would have believed me, that he was a killer? This way, the FBI was able to get him to confess.

The story received national coverage. Which was a great help to Stuart Englander. His uncle Roddy bought his serial killer screenplay for $100,000. I would have died of jealousy, but he looked so frightened every time he saw me on the street that I had to laugh.

I wish I could give you a happy ending. I can't. Two months after the shoot-out in the basement of the Boot, my mom went on new medication that helped her delusions—some. But the new drugs also made her very sleepy.

I kept going to Barnard. And even though I thought I would never go back to Ruth, I finally realized that was just foolish pride. I went back and at that first session we both cried and cried.

I was different, though, even in therapy. I trusted myself more, mentors less.

Those are good things, I know.

But Candace and Abby are gone for good, and the idea that they live in my memory provides little comfort.

I mean no disrespect to Abby and her family, but it is Candace's death that tears my heart.

For a while I tried to do everything I could to be just like her. After all, I reasoned, if I could become Candace, she would live. I cut my hair short. I was hard on waiters. I joined community-action groups. I even crossed the street the way she used to, making the cars honk and stop.

But I soon gave it up. There would never be another Candace. My own version was a mockery.

I kept her mermaid ring for over a year. I never wore it, just kept it in a drawer. But then it occurred to me that this was keeping souvenirs, and I had a kind of bad taste in my mouth about that. So one warm spring day, a year and a half after Candace's death, I went to the community garden and buried the ring, buried it deep in old Molly's rose beds.

I hadn't been in the place since Candace died. Just as I hadn't been back on the block where we had lived. But today I had a special purpose; on this day I needed to stir up painful memories.

Molly had used the ashes of her victims to make these roses so bright and healthy. It was as if the bright red flowers had taken their color from my friends' blood.

Lauren, Melita, and Jenny's remains were all buried here.

And now . . . I had added Candace's memory to the rest.

I watched the heads of the flowers sway gently in the April breeze, watched the bees buzzing around them. And then, though I still didn't feel remotely ready to say good-bye, I headed out of the garden.

Another Hodder Children's book

DEATH BY CHOCOLATE

Eric Weiner

"They're poisoned," Grace said matter-of-factly.

"Honestly, Connie," Grace told her, "if I were you I'd take those cupcakes down to the police station, let them run some lab tests on them." Instead Connie pulled out another cupcake from the bag and raised it to her lips. "Don't!" Deidre said sharply, as Connie bit deep into the cupcake's moist, chewy centre.

She let the dark flavour fill her mouth. Then she swallowed . . .

DEATH IS WATCHING

Eric Weiner

She was only halfway to the house when she heard the phone.

Jill raced into the kitchen and grabbed the red receiver that hung by the battered swinging door. "Hello?" It wasn't that she was too late. She could tell there was still someone on the line. "Hello! Hello!"

The only answer was a tiny, sinister click. And then a dial tone droned flatly in her ear . . .

ORDER FORM

Eric Weiner

0 340 65143 1   DEATH IS WATCHING   £3.50 ❑

0 340 65144 X   DEATH BY CHOCOLATE   £3.50 ❑

0 340 65145 8   DEATH IN THE DARK   £3.50 ❑

All Hodder Children's books are available at your local bookshop or newsagent, or can be ordered direct from the publisher. Just tick the titles you want and fill in the form below. Prices and availability subject to change without notice.

Hodder Children's Books, Cash Sales Department, Bookpoint, 39 Milton Park, Abingdon, OXON, OX14 4TD, UK. If you have a credit card you may order by telephone – 01235 831700.

Please enclose a cheque or postal order made payable to Bookpoint Ltd to the value of the cover price and allow the following for postage and packing: UK & BFPO – £1.00 for the first book, 50p for the second book, and 30p for each additional book ordered up to a maximum charge of £3.00. OVERSEAS & EIRE – £2.00 for the first book, £1.00 for the second book, and 50p for each additional book.

Name..

Address...

....

....

If you would prefer to pay by credit card, please complete:
Please debit my Visa/Access/Diner's Card/American Express (delete as applicable) card no:

Signature...

Expiry Date..